Murder on the Ranch!

Where was I? Under the gas tanks, catching up on my sleep. All at once Drover was right there beside me, jumping up and down and giving off that high-pitched squeal of his that kind of bores into your eardrums. You can't ignore him when he does that.

"Will you please shut up?"

"Hank, oh Hankie, it's just terrible, you wouldn't believe, hurry and wake up, I seen his tracks down on the creek, get up before he escapes!"

I pushed myself up and went nose-to-nose with the noisemaker. "Quit hopping around. Quit making all that racket. Hold still and state your business."

"Okay Hank, all right, I'll try. Oh Hank, there's been a killing right here on the ranch, and we slept through it!"

The Original Adventures of Hank the Cowdog

The Original Adventures of Hank the Cowdog

John R. Erickson

Illustrations by Gerald L. Holmes

Puffin Books

PUFFIN BOOKS
Published by the Penguin Group
Penguin Putnam Books for Young Readers,
345 Hudson Street, New York, New York 10014, U.S.A.
Penguin Books Ltd,
27 Wrights Lane, London W8 5TZ, England
Penguin Books Australia Ltd,
Ringwood, Victoria, Australia
Penguin Books Canada Ltd,
10 Alcorn Avenue, Toronto, Ontario, Canada M4V 3B2
Penguin Books (N.Z.) Ltd,
182-190 Wairau Road, Auckland 10, New Zealand

Penguin Books Ltd, Registered Offices:
Harmondsworth, Middlesex, England

First published in the United States of America
by Maverick Books, Gulf Publishing Company, 1983
Published simultaneously by Viking Children's Books and Puffin Books,
members of Penguin Putnam Books for Young Readers, 1999

12 13 14 15 16 17 18 19 20

LIBRARY OF CONGRESS CATALOGING-IN-PUBLICATION DATA
Erickson, John R.
The original adventures of Hank the Cowdog / John R. Erickson ;
illustrations by Gerald L. Holmes.
p. cm.
Originally published in series: Hank the Cowdog ; [1]
Summary: Hank the Cowdog, Head of Ranch Security, is framed
for the murder of a chicken and becomes an outlaw with the coyotes.
ISBN 0-14-130377-8 (pbk. ; alk. paper)
[1. Dogs—Fiction. 2. West (U.S.)—Fiction. 3. Humorous stories.
4. Mystery and detective stories.] I. Holmes, Gerald L., ill. II. Title.
III. Series: Erickson, John R. Hank the Cowdog ; 1.
PZ7.E72556Or 1999 [Fic]—dc21 98-41813 CIP AC

Printed in the United States of America

In memory of my mother and father,
Anna Beth and Joseph Erickson

CONTENTS

CHAPTER ONE

Bloody Murder

~~~~~~

It's me again, Hank the Cowdog. I just got some terrible news. There's been a murder on the ranch.

I know I shouldn't blame myself. I mean, a dog is only a dog. He can't be everywhere at once. When I took this job as Head of Ranch Security, I knew that I was only flesh and blood, four legs, a tail, a couple of ears, a pretty nice kind of nose that the women really go for, two bushels of hair and another half bushel of Mexican sandburs.

You add that all up and you don't get Superman, just me, good old easygoing Hank who works hard, tries to do his job, and gets very little cooperation from anyone else around here.

I'm not complaining. I knew this wouldn't be an easy job. I knew this wouldn't be an easy job. It took a special kind of dog—strong, fearless, dedicated, and above all, smart. Obviously Drover didn't fit. The job fell on my shoulders. It was my destiny. I couldn't escape the broom of history that swept through . . . anyway, I took the job.

Head of Ranch Security. Gee, I was proud of that title. Just the sound of it made my tail wag. But now this, a murder, right under my nose. I know I shouldn't blame myself, but I do.

I got the report this morning around dawn. I had been up most of the night patrolling the northern perimeter of ranch headquarters. I had heard some coyotes yapping up there and I went up to check it out. I told Drover where I was going and he came up lame all of a sudden, said he needed to rest his right front leg.

I went alone, didn't find anything. The coyotes stayed out in the pasture. I figured there were two, maybe three of them. They yapped for a couple of hours, making fun of me, calling me ugly names, and daring me to come out and fight.

Well, you know me. I'm no dummy. There's a thin line between heroism and stupidity, and I try to stay on the south side of it. I didn't go out and fight, but I answered them bark for bark, yap for yap, name for name.

The coyote hasn't been built who can out-yap Hank the Cowdog.

A little before dawn, Loper, one of the cowboys on this outfit, stuck his head out the door and bellered, "Shut up that yapping, you idiot!" I guess he thought there was only one coyote out there.

They kept it up and I gave it back to them. Next time Loper came to the door, he was armed. He fired a gun into the air and squalled, something about how a man couldn't sleep around here with all the dad-danged noise. I agreed.

Would you believe it? Them coyotes yipped louder than ever, and I had no choice but to give it back to them.

Loper came back out on the porch and fired another shot. This one came so close to me that I heard the hum. Loper must have lost his bearings or something, so I barked louder than ever to give him my position, and, you know, to let him know that I was out there protecting the ranch.

The next bullet just derned near got me. I mean, I felt the wind of it as it went past. That was enough for me. I shut her down for the night. If Loper couldn't aim any better than that, he was liable to hurt somebody.

I laid low for a while, hiding in the shelter belt, until I was sure the artillery had gone back to bed. Then I went down for a roll in the sewer, cleaned up, washed myself real good, came out feeling refreshed and ready to catch up on my sleep. Trotted down to the gas tanks and found Drover curled up in my favorite spot.

I growled him off my gunnysack. "Beat it, son. Make way for the night patrol."

He didn't want to move so I went to sterner measures, put some fangs on him. That moved him out, and he didn't show no signs of lameness either. I have an idea that where Drover is lamest is between his ears.

I did my usual bedtime ritual of walking in a tight circle around my bed until I found just exactly the spot I wanted, and then I flopped down. Oh, that felt good! I wiggled around and finally came to rest with all four paws sticking up in the air. I closed my eyes and had some wonderful twitching dreams about . . . don't recall exactly the subject matter, but most likely they were about Beulah, the neighbor's collie. I dream about her a lot.

What a woman! Makes my old heart pound just to think about her. Beautiful brown and white hair, big eyes, nose that tapers down to a point (not quite as good as mine, but so what?), and nice ears that flap when she runs.

Only trouble is that she's crazy about a spotted bird dog, without a doubt the ugliest, dumbest, worthlessest cur I ever met. What could be uglier than a spotted short-haired dog with a long skinny tail? And what could be dumber or more worthless than a dog that goes around chasing *birds*?

They call him Plato. I don't know why, except maybe because his eyes look like plates half the time, empty plates. He don't know a cow from a sow, but do you think that makes him humble? No sir. He thinks that bird-chasing is hot stuff. What really hurts, though, is that Beulah seems to agree.

Don't understand that woman, but I dream about her a lot.

Anyway, where was I? Under the gas tanks, catching up on my sleep. All at once Drover was right there beside me, jumping up and down and giving off that high-pitched squeal of his that kind of bores into your eardrums. You can't ignore him when he does that.

Well, I throwed open one eye, kept the other one shut so that I could get some halfway sleep. "Will you please shut up?"

"Hank, oh Hankie, it's just terrible, you wouldn't believe, hurry and wake up, I seen his tracks down on the creek, get up before he escapes!"

I throwed open the other eye, pushed myself up, and went nose-to-nose with the noisemaker. "Quit hopping around. Quit making all that racket. Hold still and state your business."

"Okay Hank, all right, I'll try." He tried and was none too successful, but he did get the message across. "Oh Hank, there's been a killing, right here on the ranch, and we slept through it!"

"Huh?" I was coming awake by then, and the word *killing* sent a jolt clean out to the end of my tail. "Who's been killed?"

"They hit the chickenhouse, Hank. I don't know how they got in but they did, busted in there and killed one of those big leghorn hens, killed her dead, Hank, and oh, the blood!"

Well, that settled it. I had no choice but to go back on duty. A lot of dogs would have just turned over and gone back to sleep, but I take this stuff pretty serious.

We trotted up to the chickenhouse, and Drover

kept jumping up and down and talking. "I found some tracks down by the creek. I'm sure they belong to the killer, Hank, I'm just sure they do."

"What kind of tracks?"

"Coyote."

"Hmm." We reached the chickenhouse and, sure enough, there was the hen lying on the ground, and she was still dead. I walked around the body, sniffing it good and checking the signs.

I noticed the position of the body and memorized every detail. The hen was lying on her left side, pointing toward the northeast, with one foot out and the other one curled up under her wing. Her mouth was open and it appeared to me that she had lost some tail feathers.

"Uh-huh, I'm beginning to see the pattern."

"What, tell me, Hank, who done it?"

"Not yet. Where'd you see them tracks?" There weren't any tracks around the corpse, ground was too hard. Drover took off in a run and I followed him down into the brush along the creek.

He stopped and pointed to some fresh tracks in the mud. "There they are, Hank, just where I found them. Are you proud of me?"

I pushed him aside and studied the sign,

looked it over real careful, sniffed it, gave it the full treatment. Then I raised up.

"Okay, I've got it now. It's all clear. Them's coon tracks, son, not coyote. I can tell from the scent. Coons must have attacked while I was out on patrol. They're sneaky, you've got to watch 'em every minute."

Drover squinted at the tracks. "Are you sure those are coon tracks? They sure look like coyote to me."

"You don't go by the *look,* son, you go by the *smell.* This nose of mine don't lie. If it says coon, you better believe there's a coon at the end of them tracks. And I'm fixing to clean house on him. Stay behind me and don't get hurt."

I threaded my way through the creek willows, over the sand, through the water. I never lost the scent. In the heat of a chase, all my senses come alive and point like a blazing arrow toward the enemy.

In a way I felt sorry for the coon, even though he'd committed a crime and become my mortal enemy. With me on his trail, the little guy just didn't have a chance. One of the disadvantages of being as big and deadly as I am is that you sometimes find yourself in sympathy with the other guy.

But part of being Head of Ranch Security is learning to ignore that kind of emotion. I mean, to hold down this job, you have to be cold and hard.

The scent was getting stronger all the time, and it didn't smell exactly like any coon I'd come across before. All at once I saw him. I stopped dead still and Drover, the little dummy, ran right into me and almost had a heart attack. I guess he thought I was a giant coon or something. It's hard to say what he thinks.

The coon was hiding in some bushes about five feet in front of me. I could hear him chewing on something, and that smell was real strong now.

"What's that?" Drover whispered, sniffing the air.

"Coon, what do you think?" I glanced back at him. He was shaking with fear. "You ready for some combat experience?"

"Yes," he squeaked.

"All right, here's the plan. I'll jump him and try to get him behind the neck. You come in the second wave and take what you can. If you run away like you did last time, I'll sweep the corral with you and give you a whupping you won't forget. All right, let's move out."

I crouched down and crept forward, every muscle in my highly conditioned body taut and ready for action. Five feet, four feet, three feet, two. I sprang through the air and hit right in the middle of the biggest porcupine I ever saw.

CHAPTER TWO

Quills: Just Part of the Job

It was kind of a short fight. Coming down, I seen them quills aimed up at me and tried to change course. Too late. I don't move so good in midair.

I lit right in the middle of him and *bam,* he slapped me across the nose with his tail, sure did hurt too, brought tears to my eyes. I hollered for Drover to launch the second wave but he had disappeared.

Porcupine took another shot at me but I dodged, tore up half an acre of brush, and got the heck out of there. As I limped back up to the house on pin-cushion feet, my thoughts went back to the murder scene and the evidence I had committed to memory.

It was clear now. The porcupine had had nothing at all to do with the murder because porcupines don't eat anything but trees.

Drover had found the first set of tracks he had come to and had started hollering about coyotes. I had been duped into believing the runt.

Yes, it was all clear. I had no leads, no clues, no idea who had killed the hen. What I *did* have was a face-full of porcupine quills, as well as several in my paws.

I limped up to the yard gate. As you might expect, Drover was nowhere to be seen. I sat down beside the gate and waited for Loper to come out and remove the quills.

A lot of dogs would have set up a howl and a moan. Not me. I figgered that when a dog got to be Head of Ranch Security, he ought to be able to stand some pain. It just went with the territory.

So I waited and waited and Loper didn't come out. Them quills was beginning to hurt.

The end of my nose throbbed, felt like a balloon. Made me awful restless, but I didn't whine or howl.

Pete the Barncat came along just then, had his tail stuck straight up in the air and was rubbing along the fence, coming my way. He had his usual dumb-cat expression and I could hear him purring.

He came closer. I glared at him. "Scram, cat."

He stopped, arched his back, and rubbed up against the fence. "What's that on your face?"

"Nothing you need to know about."

He rubbed and purred, then reached up and sharpened his claws on a post. "You sure look funny with all those things sticking out of your nose."

"You're gonna look funny if you don't run along and mind your own business. I'm not in the mood to take any of your trash right now."

He grinned and kept coming, started rubbing up against my leg. I decided to ignore him, look the other way and pretend he wasn't there. Sometimes that's the best way to handle a cat, let him know that you won't allow him to get you stirred up. You have to be firm with cats. Give 'em the slightest encouragement and he'll try to move in and take over.

Pete rubbed and purred. I ignored him, told myself he wasn't there. Then he brought that tail up and flicked it across the end of my nose. I curled my lip and growled. He looked up at me and did it again.

It tickled my nose, made my eyes water. I had to sneeze. I tried to fight it back but couldn't hold it. I gave a big sneeze and them quills sent fire shooting through my nose, kind of inflamed me, don't you see, and all at once I lost my temper.

I made a snap at him but he was gone, over the fence and into Sally May's yard, which is sort of off limits to us dogs even though Pete can come and go as he pleases, which ain't fair.

With the fence between us, Pete knew he was safe. He throwed a hump into his back and hissed, and what was I supposed to do then? Sing him a lullaby? Talk about the weather? No sir, I barked. I barked hard and loud, just to let that cat know that he couldn't get *me* stirred up.

The door opened and Loper stepped out on the porch. He was wearing jeans and an undershirt, no hat and no boots, and he had a cup of coffee in his hand.

"Hank! Leave the cat alone!"

I stopped and stared at him. *Leave the cat alone!* Pete grinned and walked off, purring and switching the tip of his tail back and forth.

I could have killed him.

I whined and wagged my tail and went over to the gate where Loper could see my nose. He looked up at the sky, took a drink of coffee, swatted a mosquito on his arm, looked up at the clouds again. I whined louder and jumped on the gate so that he couldn't miss seeing that old Hank, his loyal friend and protector of the ranch, had been wounded in the line of duty.

"Don't jump on the gate." He yawned and went back into the house.

Twenty minutes later he came out again, dressed for the day's work. I had waited patiently. My nose was really pounding by this time, but I didn't complain. When he came out the gate, I jumped up to greet him.

Know what he said? "Hank, you stink! Have you been in the sewer again?" And he walked on down to the corral, didn't see the quills in my nose.

At last he saw them. We were down at the corral. He shook his head and muttered, "Hank, when are you going to learn about porcupines? How many times do we have to go through this? Drover never gets quills in his nose."

Well, Drover was a little chicken and Loper just didn't understand. Nobody understood.

He got a pair of fencing pliers out of the saddle shed, threw a leg lock on me, and started pulling. It hurt. Oh it hurt! Felt like he was pulling off my whole nose. But I took it without

a whimper—well, maybe I whimpered a little bit—and we got 'er done.

Loper rubbed me behind the ears. "There, now try to stay away from porcupines." He stood up and started to dust off his jeans when he noticed the wet spot.

His eyes came up and they looked kind of wrathful. "Did you do that?"

I was well on my way to tall timber when he threw the pliers at me.

I couldn't help it. I didn't do it on purpose. The quills just got to hurting so bad that I had to let something go. Was it my fault that he had me in a leg lock and got in the way?

Make one little mistake around this ranch and they nail you to the wall.

I laid low for a while, hid in the post pile and nursed my nose. It was about ten o'clock when Sally May discovered the murdered hen.

CHAPTER THREE

An Enormous Monster

I debated for a long time about what to do next. Should I hide out and play it safe, or go on down to the chickenhouse and get blamed for something that wasn't my fault?

Curiosity got the best of me and I trotted down to see what was going on.

Drover was already there when I arrived, wagging his stub tail and trying to win a few points with his loyal dog routine. I walked up to him and said, out of the corner of my mouth, "Thanks for all the help this morning. I really appreciate it."

I think he missed the note of irony, because he said—and I mean with a straight face—he said, "That's okay, Hankie, it wasn't nothing."

Dang right it wasn't nothing.

Loper was kneeling over the hen, studying the signs. Sally May stood nearby, looking mighty unhappy about the dead chicken. Loper pushed his hat to the back of his head and stood up. His eyes went straight to me and Drover, only when I glanced around, I noticed that Drover had disappeared. It was just me, standing in the spotlight.

"Hank, if you hadn't been out barking all night, you might have prevented this. Why do you think we keep you around here?" I hung my head and tucked my tail. "Do you have any idea how much money it costs to keep you dogs around here? Seems that every time I turn around I'm having to buy another fifty-pound sack of dog food. That stuff's expensive."

Maybe this ain't the time or place to argue the point, but just for the record let me say that Co-op dog food is the cheapest you can buy. I don't know what they make it out of, hulls, straw, sawdust, anything the pigs won't eat, and then they throw in a little grease to give it a so-called flavor. Tastes like soap and about half the time it gives me an upset stomach.

The point is, I wasn't exactly eating the ranch into bankruptcy. Thought I ought to throw that in to give a more balanced view of things.

Loper went on. "We can't afford to keep you

dogs around here if you're going to let this sort of thing go on. Everybody has to earn his keep on the ranch. I don't want this to happen again."

What did he suppose *I* wanted? Sometimes I just don't understand . . . oh well.

He picked up the dead chicken by the feet and carried it down to the trash barrel. I got to admit that I watched this with some interest, since it had occurred to me that there wasn't much any of us could do for the dead chicken.

The more I thought about chicken dinner, the more my mouth watered. Couldn't get it off my mind. I like chicken about as well as any food you can name. Has a nice clean taste except for the feathers. Feathers are pretty tasteless, if you ask me, and they kind of scrape when they go down.

Sure was hungry for chicken, but I decided against it. Wouldn't look too good if I got caught eating the murder victim, after all the trouble I'd gotten into that day.

I tried to concentrate on the scene of the crime. I studied it again, went over the ground and sniffed it out. Nothing, no clues, no tracks, no scent. Could have been a coyote, a coon, a skunk, a badger, even a fox.

But there was one thing I was sure of. It wouldn't happen again, not while I was in charge of security, not as long as I could still stand up and fight for the ranch.

I saw Drover peek his head out of the machine shed. "Get some sleep, son," I told him. "Tonight we throw up a double guard, and we could get ourselves into some combat."

We slept till dark. When the moon came up, we went out on patrol, made several laps around headquarters. Everything was quiet. Off in the distance we heard a few coyotes, but they weren't anywhere close.

Must have been after midnight when Drover said his feet hurt, he wanted to rest a while. I left him in front of the chickenhouse and told him to sound the alarm if he saw anything unusual. I went on down and checked things at the corral, made the circle around the place, and ended up back at the chickenhouse about half an hour later.

Thought I'd drop in unannounced and check on Drover, make sure he was taking care of business. As I sneaked up, I could see him in the moonlight. His ears were perked. He'd take about two steps and pounce on something with his front paws. Then he'd take two more steps and pounce again.

He wasn't paying a lick of attention to the

chickenhouse. A guy could have driven a truck in there, loaded up all the hens, and been gone before Drover ever got the news.

I walked up behind him. "What are you doing?"

He screeched and headed for the machine shed. I called him back. He came out, looking all around with big eyes. "Is that you, Hank?"

"Uh-huh. What were you doing?"

"Me? Oh nuthin'."

It was then that I saw the toad frog jump. "Playing with a toad frog? On guard duty? When we got a murderer running around loose?"

He hung his head and went to wagging that stub tail of his. "I got bored, Hank."

"Sit down, son, me and you need to have a serious talk." He sat down and I marched back and forth in front of him. "Drover, I'm really disappointed in you. When you came to this ranch, you said you wanted to be a cowdog. I had misgivings at the time. I mean, you didn't look like a cowdog. But I took you on anyway and tried to teach you the business. Can you imagine how it breaks my heart to come up here and find you playing with a dad-gummed toad frog?"

His head sank lower and lower, and he started to sniffle.

"If you had gone into any other line of work,

playing with a frog would be all right, but a cow-dog is something special. You might say we're the elite. We have to be stronger, braver, and tougher than any brand of dog in the world. It's a special calling, Drover, it ain't for the common run of mutts."

He started crying.

"Drover, there's only one thing that keeps you from being a good cowdog."

"What is it, Hank?"

"You're worthless."

"Oh no," he squalled, "don't say it! It hurts too much."

"But it's true. I've tried to be patient, I've tried to teach you, I've tried to be a good example."

"I know."

"But it hasn't worked. You're just as worthless today as you were the first time I saw you."

"Oh-h-h!"

"You're just a chickenhearted little mutt, is what you are, and I don't think you'll ever make a cowdog."

"Yes I will, Hank, I just need some time."

"Nope. Duty's duty. I got no choice but to let you go."

He broke down and sobbed. "Oh Hank, I got no place to go, no friends, no family. Nobody wants a chickenhearted mutt. Give me just three more chances."

"Can't do it, Drover, sorry."

"Two more?"

"Nope."

"One more?"

I paced back and forth. It was one of the most difficult decisions of my career and I didn't want to rush into it.

"All right, one more chance. But one more dumb stunt and you're finished, and I mean forever. Now dry your eyes, shape up, pay attention to your business, and concentrate on being unworthless."

"Okay, Hank." He started jumping up and down and going around in circles. "You won't be sorry. No more frogs for me. I'll guard that chickenhouse and give my life if necessary." —

"That's the spirit. I'm going to make the rounds again. If you see anything suspicious, give a holler."

I started off on my rounds and left him sitting in front of the chickenhouse door. I was down at the feed room, checking for coons, when I heard him sound the alarm.

I turned on my incredible speed and went tearing up the hill. I have several speeds, don't you see: slow, normal, and incredible. I save the last one back for special emergencies. When I turn on the incredible speed, I appear as a streak of color moving across the ground. Anything that gets in my way is knocked aside, often destroyed, and I'm not talking about little stuff either. I mean trees, posts, big rocks, you name it.

As I was streaking up the hill, I met Drover.

"Hank, I seen him, he's up there, my gosh!"

I had to slow down. "Give me a description."

"Big, Hank, and I mean *BIG*, huge, enormous. Black and white, gigantic tail that whishes through the air, long pointed tongue that flicks out at you, and horns growing out of his head."

"Good grief," I whispered, "what is it?"

"It's a *monster*, Hank, a gen-u-wine monster!"

I stopped to think it over. I'd never tangled with a monster before. "You think I can whip him?"

"I don't know, Hank. But if anybody can, it's you."

"You're right. Okay, here's the plan. I'll go in the first wave, make the first contact. We'll hold you in reserve. If I holler for help, you come running, get in there with them teeth of yours and bite something. Got that?"

"I got it."

I took a deep breath. "And Drover, if I don't

come back from this one, you'll have to go on alone. Take care of the ranch and be brave."

It was kind of a touching moment, me and Drover standing there in the moonlight just before the big battle. I said good-bye and loped up the hill.

I stopped and peered into the gloom. At first I couldn't see anything, but then my eyes fell on a huge shadowy thing standing right in front of the chickenhouse door.

Drover hadn't exaggerated. It was a horned monster, all right, and he was fixing to bust down the door and start killing chickens. I didn't have a moment to waste. It was now or never, him or me, glory or death. I bared my fangs and attacked.

First contact was made only a matter of seconds after I launched the attack. The monster must have heard me coming, cause he kicked the tar out of me and sent me rolling. I leaped up and charged again but this time I made it through, sank my teeth into him and gave him a ferocious bite. He slung me around, but I hung on.

He was big, all right, big as a house. I figgered he stood, oh, fourteen feet tall at the shoulder, had three eyes, a long forked tongue, and a tail with deadly stingers on the end of it, also horns that glowed in the dark. And tusks. Did I mention that? Big long tusks growing out of the side of his

mouth, the kind that could rip a dog to shreds.
Green slobber dripped out of his mouth and his
eyes were red.

It was a fight to the death. "Come on, Drover,
attack!" I set up a howl to alert the house. I would
need all the help I could get.

I'll give Drover credit. He came tearing out of

the weeds, yapping at the top of his lungs, and got within three feet of the monster before he veered off and headed for the machine shed.

The lights came on down at the house. The door slammed and I heard Loper running toward me. I hoped he had the gun. I was getting beat up and tired. I wasn't sure I could keep up the fight much longer.

The gun exploded, lit up the night. The monster ran and I started after him, ready to give him the *coop de grass,* as we say, but Loper called me back. I figgered he didn't want to risk losing the Head of Ranch Security, which seemed pretty sensible to me.

So I went back to him, limping on all four legs at once because they all hurt, and so did everything else. Wagging my tail, I went up to him, ready for my reward.

I didn't get no reward. To make a long story short, Drover had sent me into battle against the milk cow and I got cursed for it.

I thought very seriously about terminating Drover—I mean his life, not his job—but I couldn't find him in the machine shed. So I dragged my battered carcass down to the gas tanks and curled up on my gunnysack bed.

I could have sworn that was a monster.

CHAPTER FOUR

The Boxer

I slept late the next morning. To be real honest about it, I didn't wake up till sometime in the early afternoon. Guess all that monster fighting kind of wore me down.

What woke me up was the sound of the flatbed pickup rattling up to the gas tank, right in front of my bedroom. Loper got out and started filling the pickup. He looked at me, gave his head a shake, and said something under his breath. I tried to read his lips but couldn't make out what he said. Probably wasn't the Pledge of Allegiance.

Slim went around to the front of the pickup and opened up the hood. I was just getting up, right in the middle of a nice stretch, when I heard him say, "Hank, come here, boy."

Geeze, at last a friendly voice. How long had it been since someone had spoken to me in a kind voice? In my job, nobody ever says a word when you do something right, only when you make a mistake, and then you hear plenty about it.

I trotted around to the front of the pickup—limped, actually, because I was pretty stove up from the battle—wagged my tail and said howdy. Slim bent down and rubbed me behind the ears.

"Good dog," he said.

Good dog! I just melted on those words, rolled over on my back, and kicked all four legs in the air. It's amazing what a few kind words and a smile can do for a dog. Even as hardboiled as I am, which is something you have to be in my line of work, I respond to kindness.

Slim rubbed me in that special place at the bottom of my ribs, the one that's somehow hooked up to my back leg. I've never understood the mechanics of it, but if a guy scratches me there it makes my back leg start kicking.

Slim scratched and I kicked. Felt good and made Old Slim laugh. Then he told me to sit. I sat and tried to shake hands. Shaking hands is one of the many tricks I've learned over the years, and I can usually count on it to delight an audience of people.

But Slim didn't notice. He reached under the hood, pulled out the dipstick, and wiped it off on my ear. "Good dog." And that was it. I waited around for some more scratching or handshaking, but he seemed to forget that I was there. He slammed the hood and stepped on my paw. "Oops, sorry, Hank, get out of the way."

The sweet moments in this life are fleeting. You have to enjoy them to the fullest when they come, before some noodle steps on you and tells you to get out of the way.

Slim and Loper got into the pickup, and Loper said, "Don't you dogs try to follow us."

He gunned the motor and pulled away from the gas tank. Drover suddenly appeared out of nowhere and hopped up into the back of the pickup.

"Come on, Hank, we're supposed to go."

In the back of my mind I knew that wasn't right, but I didn't have time to think about it. I chased the pickup until it slowed down for the big hill in front of the house, and jumped up in the back.

"Where we going?" I asked.

Drover gave me that famous empty-headed look of his, the one where you can gaze into his eyes and see all the way to the end of his tail, and there's nothing in between. "Beats me, but I bet we're going somewhere."

Loper drove up to the mailbox and turned left. If he had turned right, it would have meant that we were going to the pasture. A left turn meant only one thing: we were going to town. And that meant only one thing: Loper was going to be mad as thunder when he found out we'd jumped in the back and hitched a ride.

But what the heck? You can't be safe and cautious all the time. If you're too timid in this life, you'll miss out on all the fun and adventure. You'll just stay home and snap at the flies, and when you get to be an old dog, you'll look back on your life and think, "All these years I've been on this earth, and I've never done anything but snap at flies."

And you'll regret that, when the opportunity came up, you didn't sneak a ride into town.

Drover curled up behind the cab and watched the scenery go by. I sat on my haunches, closed my eyes, and just let the wind flap my ears around. Felt good, restful. There for a little while I forgot all my cares and responsibilities.

That lasted until we got to the highway. Loper pulled onto the blacktop and started picking up speed. The wind began to sting and my ears flapped a little harder than I like them to flap, and the crumbs of alfalfa hay on the pickup bed started to swirl.

I laid down beside Drover. "Say, before I forget, I want to thank you for all the help you gave me last night with that monster."

He gave me a shy grin. "Oh, that's okay. It was the least I could do."

"It sure as heck was. If you'd done any leaster, you'd have been fighting for the other side."

The shy grin disappeared. "You mad about something?"

"Forget it." I didn't want to talk. Alfalfa leaves were getting into my mouth. I slept all the way to town.

Next thing I knew, we had slowed down and were coasting down Main Street. I sat up and took in the sights: a bunch of stores and street lights, several stop signs, couple of town dogs loafing around, and a big tumbleweed rolling down the middle of the street.

Loper drove into a parking place in front of the Waterhole Cafe, beside two or three other pickups that looked like cowboy rigs. When he got out and saw us back there, he gave us the tongue-lashing I had expected. It was no worse than usual, not bad enough to make me regret that we'd hitched a ride to town.

He told us to sit, be good, and don't bark.

Then he and Slim went into the Waterhole.

For five or ten minutes we concentrated on being good, which was a real drag. Then I heard Drover go, "Ps-s-s-st!" He jerked his head toward the pickup that was parked next to us. In the back end, fast asleep, was a big ugly boxer dog. We both moved to the side of the pickup bed and stared at him.

He must have felt our eyes because after a bit his head came up, and he glowered at us with a wicked expression on his face.

"What are you staring at?"

"Just looking at the sights," I said. "What's your name?"

"Puddin' Tane, ask me again and I'll tell you the same."

I guess Drover didn't understand what that meant, so he asked, "What's your name?"

"John Brown, ask me again and I'll knock you down."

Drover gave me a puzzled look, and I said, "How come they've got you chained up?" He was tied to the headache racks of the pickup with a piece of chain.

"So I won't kill any dogs."

"You kill dogs, no fooling?" Drover asked.

"Just for drill. I prefer bigger stuff."

That sort of ended the conversation. Puddin' Tane went back to sleep and I got involved with a couple of noisy flies that were bothering my ears. Took a few snaps at 'em but didn't get anything.

Next thing I knew, Drover said, "What would you do if we peed on your tires?"

The boxer's head came up real slow, and he turned them wicked eyes on little Drover. "What did you say?"

"I said, what would you do if we peed on your tires?"

"Uh, Drover . . ." It made me a little uneasy, the way he was talking about *we*.

The boxer sat up. "I'd tear off your legs and wring your neck."

"But how could you do that when you're chained up?"

"Drover."

The boxer lifted one side of his mouth and unveiled a set of long white teeth. "I'd bust the chain.

"It looks pretty stout to me."

"*Drover.*"

"It ain't stout enough."

"Just curious," said Drover. Big-and-Ugly went back to sleep and I got back to them flies.

One of them was big and green, also a little slow on the draw. I waited for my shot and snapped. Got the little booger! Then I had to spit him out real quick. Boy, did he taste foul.

Seemed to me I heard water running somewhere. I glanced around and saw Big-and-Ugly's head come up. He'd heard it too.

Drover had just wiped out the left rear tire and was going toward the front one. Seemed to me this was poor judgment on Drover's part.

The boxer sprang to his feet. "Get away from that tire, runt! No two-bit cowdog is going to mess up my tires!"

I didn't like his tone of voice. I got up and wandered to the side of the pickup. "Say there, partner, maybe I didn't hear you right. You weren't suggesting that there's any two-bit cowdogs around here, were you?"

"I ain't suggesting, Buddy, I'm saying. You're a couple of two-bit cowdogs."

"Do you mean that as an insult or a compliment?"

"Cowdog don't mean but one thing to me: sorry and two-bit."

I took a deep breath. "Oh dear. Drover, the dust seems kind of bad all of a sudden. Why don't you wet down that other tire."

He grinned, hiked up his leg, and let 'er rip.

The boxer went nuts when he saw that. All at once his fangs were flashing in the sunlight. He lunged against the chain and started barking—big, deep roar of a bark, so loud you could feel it bouncing off your face.

I waited for him to shut up. "You want to take back what you said about cowdogs?" He lunged against the chain and slashed the air about six inches from the end of my nose. "Guess not."

I hopped down, skipped around to the right side of the boxer's pickup, and wiped out the front and back tires. Drover and I met at the front, swapped sides, and gave each tire a second coat.

Big-and-Ugly went berserk. He fought against the chain and roared. "Let me at 'em, I'll kill 'em, just let me at 'em!"

Drover and I finished the job and hopped back into the pickup bed. When the cafe door burst open, we were, ahem, fast asleep. Slim, Loper, and the boxer's master stormed out.

"What's going on out here? You dogs . . ."

"It's my dog, Loper, he's making all the racket. Bruno, shut up! You're disturbing the whole town."

I sat up and opened my eyes. Bruno was getting a good scolding from his master. He whined and wagged his stump tail and tried to explain what had happened. But his master didn't understand. (This seems to be a common trait in masters.)

"Now you lie down and be quiet. I don't want to hear another peep out of you. You know better than that."

The men went back inside. I waited a minute and then gave Drover the coast-is-clear sign. We got up and went over to the edge of the pickup. Bruno was lying flat, with his eyes wide open and a couple of fangs showing beneath his lips. He was trembling with rage.

"Drover, you ever seen an uglier dog than that one?"

He giggled. "No, never did."

"Me neither. Can you imagine what his mother must have looked like?"

A growl came from deep in Bruno's throat.

"I don't like his pointed ears," said Drover.

"You know why they're pointed, don't you? When boxers are born, they have such big floppy ears that a surgeon has to cut off two yards of hide. And then they whack off the tail, and then they put the pup's face into a shop vice and mash it until it looks just like Bruno's."

"No kidding?"

"Yup. And as you might expect, it affects the brain too, mashes it down to the size of a dog biscuit." The growl in Bruno's throat was growing louder. "That's why boxers are so dumb, brain's been smallered. It's the mark of the breed. They tell me that you can't get papers on a boxer unless he's too dumb to walk across the street. They give 'em a test, see, and all the ones that flunk become registered boxers."

By this time the growl had become a steady roar.

"And that's why you never see boxers work cattle, just too frazzling dumb to hold down a steady job."

Bruno's eyes were cloudy, as if they were filled with smoke from a fire burning inside. His teeth were snapping together. Maybe he was crushing imaginary bones.

"Why would anybody want a dog that was so big and dumb and ugly?" Drover asked.

"I've wondered about that myself," said I, "and the only answer I can come up with is that maybe if a guy had a piece of log chain that he didn't know what to do with, he'd buy a boxer to hang it on."

That did it. Bruno erupted again and lunged at us, his mouth wide open and full of jagged teeth. I got a real good look at his tonsils, which appeared to be a little inflamed.

I jerked my head at Drover and we was both sending up a line of Z's when the cowboys came out again.

"Bruno, what in the world! Bad dog, bad dog! Why can't you just lie still and shut up like these other dogs?" Bruno whimpered. "Well, I guess I'd better go. Bruno's on a snort. See y'all later."

When the pickup drove off, me and Drover sat up and grinned and waved good-bye to our new friend. Bruno was so mad his eyes were crossed and foam dripped off his chops.

That's what makes being a cowdog worthwhile. Teamwork.

CHAPTER FIVE

Another Bloody Murder

When we crossed the cattleguard that put us back on the ranch, I felt a change come over me.

In town I had been just another happy-go-lucky dog without a care in the world. But back on the ranch, I felt that same crushing sense of responsibility that's known to people in high places, such as presidents, prime ministers, emperors, and such. Being Head of Ranch Security is a great honor but also a dreadful burden.

I remembered the chickenhouse murder. I still didn't have any suspects, or I had too many suspects, maybe that was it. Everyone was a suspect, well, everyone but the milk cow, and I had pretty muchly scratched her off the list. And the porcupine, since they only eat trees.

But every other creature on the ranch was under the shadow of suspicion. Except Drover. He was too chicken to kill a chicken.

When we got home, I trotted up to the chicken-house and went over the whole thing in my mind. While I was sitting there, lost in thought, a chicken came up and pecked me on the tail. Scared the fool out of me just for a second. I snarled at her and made her squawk and flap her wings.

That's another thing about this job. Every day, every night you put your life on the line, and for what? A bunch of idiot birds that would just as soon peck you on the tail as tell you good morning. Sometimes you wonder if it's worth it, and all that keeps you going is dedication to duty.

In the end, that's what separates the top echelon of cowdogs from the common rubble . . . rabble, whatever the word is, anyway the dogs that don't give a rip, is what I'm saying.

Well, I had nothing to work with, no evidence, no case. There wasn't a thing I could do until the killer struck again. I could only hope that me and Drover could catch him in the act.

I decided to change my strategy. Instead of throwing a guard around the chickenhouse, we would use the stake-out approach.

"Stake-out" is a technical term which we use in this business. Webster defines "stake" as "a length of wood or metal pointed at one end for driving into the ground." It comes from the Anglo-Saxon word *staca*, akin to the Danish *staak*.

"Out" is defined as "away from, forth from, or removed from a place, position, or situation." It comes from the Middle English *ut*.

That's about as technical as I can make it.

In layman's terms, a stake-out is basically a trap. You leave the chickenhouse unguarded, don't you see, and watch and wait and wait and watch until the villain makes his move, and then you swoop in and get him.

It's pretty simple, really, when you get used to the terminology.

At dark, me and Drover staked the place out. We hid in some tall weeds maybe thirty feet from the chickenhouse.

Time sure did drag. The first couple of hours we heard coyotes howling off in the pastures. Drover kept looking around with big eyes. I thought he might try to slip off to the machine shed, but he didn't. After a while, he laid his head down on his paws and went to sleep.

I could have kept him awake, I mean, pulled rank and *demanded* that he stay awake, but I thought, what the heck, the little guy probably needed the sleep. I figgered I could keep watch and wake him up when the time came for action.

Then I fell asleep, but the funny thing about it was that I dreamed I was awake, sitting here and standing guard. I kept saying, "Hank, are you still awake?" And Hank said, "Sure I am. If I was asleep, you and I wouldn't be talking like this, would we?" And I said, "No, I suppose not."

Seems to me it's kind of a waste of good sleep to dream about what you were doing when you were awake, but that's what happened.

I heard something squawk, and I said, "Hank, what's that?"

"Nuthin."

"You sure?"

"Sure I'm sure. You're wide awake and watching the stake-out, aren't you?"

"I think so, yes."

"Then stop worrying.

The squawking went on and the next thing I knew, Drover was jumping up and down. "Hank, oh Hank, he's back, murder, help, blood, we fell asleep, oh my gosh, Hank, wake up!"

"Huh? I ain't asleep." And right then my eyes popped open and I woke up. "Dang the luck, I *was* asleep! I was afraid of that."

We dashed out of the weeds and found a body south of the chickenhouse door. The M.O. was the same. (There's another technical term, M.O. It stands for *Modus of Operationus,* which means *how it was done.* We shorten it to M.O.)

A pattern began to emerge. The killer had struck twice and both times he had killed a white leghorn hen. (Actually, that might not have been a crucial point because there weren't any other-colored hens on the place, but I mention it to demonstrate the kind of deep thinking that goes into solving a case of this type. You can't overlook a single detail, even those that don't mean anything.)

But the most revealing clue was that the murderer hadn't dragged his victim off. That meant that he hadn't killed for food, but only for the sport of it. In other words, we had a pathagorical killer on the loose.

This was very significant, the first big break in the case. At last I had an M.O. that narrowed the suspects down to coyotes, coons, skunks, badgers, foxes . . . rats, it hadn't eliminated anybody and I was right back where I started.

I hunkered down and studied the body. It was still warm. Warm chicken. My mouth began to water and I noticed a rumble in my stomach. This fresh evidence was pointing the case in an entirely new direction.

"Uh Drover, why don't you run on and get some sleep? You've had a tough day."

"Oh, I'm awake now."

"You look sleepy."

"I do?"

"Yes, you do, awful sleepy. Your eyes seem kind of baggy."

"Don't you think we should sound the alarm?"

"Not just yet. I need to do a little more study on the corpse." My stomach growled real loud.

Drover perked his ears. "What was that?"

"I didn't hear anything."

He waited and listened. I concentrated on making my stomach shut up. You can do that, you know, control your body with your mind, only it didn't work this time. My stomach growled again, sounded like a rusty gate hinge.

"What *is* that?"

"Rigor mortis," I said. "Chickens do that. Run along now and get some sleep. We've got a big day ahead of us."

"Well, okay." He started off and heard my stomach again. He turned around and twisted his head and stared at me. "Was that *you*?"

"Don't be absurd. Good night, Drover."

He shrugged and went on down to the gas tanks. I gave him plenty of time to bed down, get comfortable, snap at a few mosquitoes, and fall asleep. My mouth was watering so much that it was dripping off my chin.

When everything was real quiet, I snatched up the body, loped out into the horse pasture, and began my postmortem investigation. It was very interesting.

I didn't hurry this part of the investigation. I labored over my work for several hours and fell into a peaceful sleep.

When I awoke it was bright daylight. I could feel the rays of the sun warming my coat. I glanced around, trying to remember where I was, and when I figured it out, my heart almost stopped beating.

I was lying in the center of a circle of white feathers, and several more feathers were clinging to my mouth and nose. My belly bulged, and Sally May was standing over me, a look of horror on her face.

"Hank! *You're* the one! Oh Hank, how could you!"

Huh? No wait, there had been a mistake. I had only . . . well, you see, I just . . . the chicken was already dead and I thought . . . hey, listen, I can explain everything . . .

It must have looked pretty bad, me lying there in the midst of all that damaging evidence. Sally May headed down to the house, swinging her arms and walking fast.

I didn't know what to do. If I ran, it would look bad. If I stayed, it would look bad. No matter what I did, it would look bad. Maybe eating the dern chicken had been a mistake.

I was still sitting there, mulling over my next

course of action, when Sally May returned with her husband.

"There, look. You see who's been killing the chickens? *Your dog!*"

I whapped my tail against the ground and put on my most innocent face. Loper and I had been through a lot together. Surely he would know that his Head of Ranch Security wasn't a common chicken-killing dog. He had to trust me.

But I could see his face harden, and I knew I was cooked. "Hank, you bad dog. I never would have thought you'd do something like this."

I didn't! It was all a mistake, I'd been framed.

"Come here, Hank." I crawled over to him. He picked up the chicken head which was lying on the ground. I hadn't eaten it because I've found that beaks are hard to swaller. He tied a piece of string around the head and tied it around my neck. "There. You wear that chicken head until it falls off. Maybe that'll help you remember that killing hens doesn't pay around here."

They left, talking in low voices and shaking their heads. I tried to bite the string and get that thing off my neck, but I couldn't do it. I was feeling mighty low, mighty blue. I was ashamed of myself, but also outraged at the injustice of it.

I headed down to the corral to find Drover.

Instead, I ran into Pete the Barncat, just the guy I didn't want to see. He was sunning himself in front of the saddle shed—in other words, *loafing*, which is what he does about ninety-five percent of the time. The mice were rampant down at the feed barn, but Pete couldn't work a mouse patrol into his busy schedule. It interfered with his loafing. That's a cat for you.

He saw me before I saw him. He yawned and a big grin spread across his mouth. "Nice necklace you got on, Hankie. Where could a feller buy one of those?"

You have to be in the mood for Pete, and I wasn't. I made a dive for him and he escaped instant death by a matter of inches. He hissed and ran, and I fell in right behind him.

I chased him around the corrals. He hissed and I barked. There were several horses in the west lot and they all started bucking and kicking up their heels. It was my lousy luck that Slim happened to be riding one of them—a two-year-old colt, as I recall—and he started yelling.

"Hank, get outa here! Whoa, Sinbad, easy bronc!"

Nobody around here ever yells at the cat. Why? I don't know, I just don't understand.

I gave up the chase. I would settle accounts

with Pete some other day. I loped over to the gas tank, looking for Drover. He heard me coming, sat up, saw the chicken head around my neck, turned tail, and sprinted for the machine shed as fast as he could go.

"Drover, wait, it's me, Hank!"

He kept going. I guess he didn't want to get involved with a criminal.

I went down to the gas tank and lay down. Boy, I felt low. I tried to sleep but didn't have much luck. That chicken head was starting to smell, and it reminded me all over again of the injustice of my situation.

Off in the distance, I could hear Pete. He was still up in the tree he had climbed to escape my attack, and he was singing a song called "Mommas, Don't Let Your Puppies Grow Up to Be Cowdogs." Now and then he would stop singing, and I would hear him laughing. Really got under my skin.

I lay there brooding for a long time. Then I pushed myself up and all of a sudden it was clear what I would have to do. They had left me no choice.

I took one last look at my bedroom there under the gas tank, and started up the hill. As I passed by the machine shed door, Drover stuck his head out.

"Psst! Where you going?"

I trotted past. "I'm leaving."

He crept out, glanced around to see if anybody was watching, and came after me. "Leaving?"

"That's right. I quit, I resign."

His jaw dropped. "You can't do that."

"You just watch me. This chicken head was the last straw. I'm fed up with this place. I'm moving on."

"Moving . . . where you going?"

"I don't know yet. West, toward the setting sun."

He was quiet for a minute, then, "I'll go with you."

"No you won't."

"How come?"

"Because, Drover, I'm starting a new life. I'm gonna become an outlaw."

The breath whistled through his throat. "An outlaw!"

"That's right. They've driven me to it. I tried to run this ranch, but it just didn't work. I'm going back to the wild. One of these days, they'll be sorry."

"But, Hank . . ."

"Good-bye, Drover. Take care of things. I'm sorry it has to end this way. Next time we meet, I won't be Hank the Cowdog. I'll be Hank the Outlaw. So long."

And with that, I trotted off to a new life as a criminal, outcast, nomad, and wild dog.

CHAPTER SIX

Buzzards

I made my way north, away from headquarters and up into the canyon country. If a dog was going to go back to the wild, that was the place to go.

Funny, how good it felt walking away from everything—the job, the responsibility, the constant worry. When I crossed the road there by the mailbox, I felt free for the first time in years.

On the other side of the road, I stopped and looked back. Drover had followed me about a hundred yards and stopped. He was watching. Maybe he thought I would change my mind and go back. Maybe he was waiting for me to tell him to come on.

I didn't. I ran my eyes over the ranch I had

loved and protected for so many years, waved farewell to Drover, and went on my way.

I wondered how Loper and Slim and Sally May would react when they figgered out that I had resigned and moved on. I had an idea they'd be sorry. They'd realize how they'd done me wrong and misjudged me and accused me of terrible things I didn't do. I mean, all I did was eat a dead chicken, and she wasn't a bit deader when I finished than when I started.

Maybe they'd cry. Why not? A lot of people cry over their dogs. They tell me that when Lassie and Rin Tin Tin were big on TV, people used to cry when they thought Lassie was in a jam she couldn't get out of, and when Rinny had got himself chewed up by a bear and it appeared that he wouldn't pull out of it.

People never realize just how important a dog is until it's too late. In life we get yelled at and cursed and kicked around, but when we're gone, people wish they had us back.

Yeah, they'd cry when they found out that old Hank had moved on, and they'd cry even harder when it dawned on them that their ranch was being protected—and I mean so-called protected—by Pete the cat and Drover the chickenhearted.

That would wring tears out of a bodark post.

Yep, they'd cry and they'd say, "Oh, I wish we had Hankie back! He had his faults but he was a good honest dog. It just won't be the same around here without him."

Around sundown, they'd walk out into the pasture and call, "Here Hank, come on Hankie, here boy!"

And you know what? I'd be up in them canyons, eating fresh meat instead of Co-op dog food, listening to the sounds of nature, and enjoying pure peace and freedom.

I'd hear 'em calling my name, begging me to come back, but I wouldn't go. They'd had their chance. I'd tried to go straight and live within the law but they'd drove me to drastic measures, drove me to follow the owl-hoot trail and become an outlaw.

Next morning, they'd get in the pickup and go driving around, checking all the spots where I used to hang out: the sewer, the gas tanks, the corral, the creek. But I wouldn't be there.

Then they'd drive over to the neighbor's place. "Anybody seen Hank? We've lost our cowdog. No? Well, we're offering a five-hundred-dollar reward to anybody who finds him."

Then they'd start driving through the pastures, honking the horn and calling, "Hank, here boy! Come on home, Hankie, we miss you. We're sorry for everything we've done. We'll do anything if you'll just come home."

Laying off in them canyons, I'd hear 'em calling. Peeking through the rocks, I'd see 'em driving slow across the pasture. But I wouldn't go back. Injustice had changed me, turned me bitter and snapped something inside me.

Anyway, that's what I was thinking about when I turned my back on the ranch forever and hit the owl-hoot trail.

They say you're not supposed to feel good about other people's misfortunes, but I got to admit that it gave me considerable wicked pleasure to know that I had left 'em weeping, and that with me gone the ranch was gonna fall apart real quick.

That's the kind of satisfaction that dog food and a flea collar just won't buy.

Must have been late afternoon when I reached the wild country, up near the head of one of them canyons. It was pretty hot down there, not much breeze. The canyon walls rose up a hundred feet in the air and a couple of buzzards floated in the sky overhead.

I was pretty tired and my feet was kind of sore from walking over the rocks, so when I found a little spring of water, I jumped in and rolled around. It was pleasant but not nearly as satisfying as a roll in the sewer.

That was one thing about my old life that I would miss. I always looked forward to the middle of the day when me and Drover used to go down to the place where the septic tank overflowed, hop in, and splash and roll around with our paws in the air and then get out and have a good old fashioned head-to-tail shake.

You can say what you want about spring water, but if you ask me, it ain't near as refreshing or healthful as good old septic tank water. And I always liked the deep rich manly smell of it. A dog ought to smell like a dog, seems to me, and I never had no desire to be one of those town dogs that get their hair clipped and their toenails painted and get sprayed all over with that stinking perfume stuff. Perfume gives me a headache and stops up my nose.

Anyway, that spring pool wasn't as refreshing as the sewer would have been, but I managed to cool myself down and satisfy my thirst. I wallered around in it for ten or fifteen minutes, and when I was ready to get out, I noticed that I had some company.

Those buzzards that had been floating around

the rim of the canyon had dropped in for a visit, two of 'em. They were perched on the ground near the edge of the pool, staring at me.

I showed 'em some fangs right away. I mean, I try to be friendly and all of that, but there's just something about a buzzard that don't sit right with me. Maybe it's because they're so ugly. Looks ain't everything in this life, unless you happen to look like a turkey buzzard, and then they're pretty crucial. It's hard to be friendly to something that ugly.

I gave 'em a growl. They bent their necks forward and stared at me. Then Wallace, the older of the two, said, "We thought maybe you was dead."

"Thinking gets birds like you in trouble. Run along, I got things to do."

They didn't move, so I stepped out on dry land and shook myself. Throwed water all over Wallace. He dropped his wings and took a couple of steps backward.

"He ain't dead, junior. You made a mistake."

I tell you, he's d-d-dead, Pa, I just know he-he-he is." Junior seemed to have a little studder problem. "When I pick up a s-s-signal, something's du-du-du-dead. Remember that ground squirrel? I picked him up at five hundred y-y-yards, and what did *you* su-say?"

Wallace frowned and squinted one eye. "I don't recall. What did I say?"

"You su-su-said I was su-seeing things, seeing things. You said my eyes was h-h-h-hooked up to my b-b-b-b-b-b . . ."

"Belly, uh, huh, it's coming back now."

"And you s-s-said I didn't have enough experience and when I g-g-got as old as you, old as you, m-maybe I'd amount to s-s-something."

"I was just trying to be optimistic, son, you can't blame me for that." Wallace burped and the whole canyon went sour. "Dang, I'm hungry."

"I'm t-t-telling you, Pa, he's du-du-du-dead. I picked up the s-s-signals, signals."

They moved a little closer and looked me over real careful. "Junior, if he's dead, how come he crawled out of that water hole?"

"Bu-beats me."

"And how come his eyes are open and he's looking back at us?"

"Bu-beats me, but he's dead."

"Maybe so, son. I never claimed to know everything."

"You du-did too, yesterday m-m-morning."

"All right, all right, I take it back. Hey!" His head shot up in the air. "I'm starting to pick up the signals now. He *is* dead, you're right!"

"Told you s-s-so."

They came toward me. I watched 'em and lifted my lip on the right side.

"Whoa, Junior, hold it, son! Did you see that lip go up? Did you see them teeth? Look there, son, see what I'm saying?"

Junior stretched out his skinny neck and studied me for a minute. "That d-don't mean n-nuthin. I'll p-p-p-prove it, prove it."

And with that, Junior marched up and pecked me on top of the head. As you might imagine, I didn't care for that and I took a snap at Junior and relieved him of a double handful of feathers. The buzzards went running for cover. The old man tripped over a rock, went down, hopped up, and kept going, looking back over his wing the whole time.

"I told you he wasn't dead!"

"But Pa . . ."

"I told you once, I told you twice, I told you three times!"

"But Pa . . ."

"You're gonna keep fooling around and get us hurt one of these days."

"But Pa . . . what's that around his neck?"

"Huh?" They were back to looking at me again.

"That's where the s-s-signal's coming from, that thing around his n-n-n-n-n, under his chin."

Old Wallace's eyes popped open and a smile came over his beak. "I believe you're right, son. It's a chicken head!" Wallace put on a pleasant face (for a buzzard) and came waddling over to me. "Hi there. You new around here?"

"Maybe."

"I'm Wallace, this here's Junior, and we was just . . . what would you take for that chicken head?"

"What you got?"

They went into a huddle, then the old man said, "Tell you what, neighbor, times are hard right now. My eyes is going bad on me and Junior's a little on the simple-minded side of things, and we haven't had a good meal in three days. We sure are hungry and we sure could use a chicken head right now, till our luck changes. We'd have to take it on credit, is the long and short of it."

"We'd d-do you a fu-fu-fu-favor sometime, sometime."

Wallace nodded his head. "Yes we would, we surely would, because we never forget a good deed."

I thought it over. Seemed to me that trading a stinking chicken head for a buzzard's good will was about an even swap. You couldn't take either one of them to the bank.

"Tell you what, boys, if you can chew the string in half, I'll let you have the head."

Their eyes lit up and Junior started toward me, only the old man slapped him across the mouth with his wing. "I'll handle this. You just stand by for further orders."

Wallace waddled over and squinted at the string. He leaned out his neck and took a bite, got my ear instead of the string. I yelped and jumped away.

"I'm sorry, dang I'm sorry. It's my eyes. Let me try again."

"All right, try again, but leave the ear where it sits."

He tried again, and this time he found the string and chewed it in half. Just as soon as the head hit the ground, Junior made a dive for it, swooped it up in his beak, and ran off.

The old man went after him, flapping his wings and stumbling over rocks and things. "Junior, you come back here! Junior!"

They fought over it for five minutes. First Junior had it, then Wallace had it, then they got so busy fighting that it fell to the ground. A chicken hawk swooped down and picked it up, and that was the last they ever saw of their supper.

That stopped the fight. "See what you done!" Wallace squawked.

"*You* d-d-done it cause you're so g-g-greedy, greedy."

It was about dark by this time, so I found me a comfortable spot and curled up for the night. Junior and Wallace argued back and forth for another hour, until at last they shut up and we had some peace and quiet. I was drifting off to sleep when I heard Junior's voice.

"P-Pa?"

"What?"

"I'm h-hungry."

"You oughta be, after the way you acted."

Silence. "P-Pa?"

"What!"

"You ever eat a d-d-dog?"

I raised my head. "The first son of a buck that comes creeping around me in the night is gonna get his legs tore off, one by one."

Didn't hear another sound out of them birds for the rest of the night, and they didn't stay for breakfast.

CHAPTER SEVEN

True Love

Actually there wasn't any breakfast. And then there wasn't any lunch. Along toward the middle of the afternoon, it occurred to me that if I wanted to eat, I would have to get out and hustle some grub.

I left camp and lit out north, figuring I would scout the head of the canyon. I hadn't gone very far when I stopped dead in my tracks. I heard something, kind of a clanking sound.

I slipped behind a bush and studied the country ahead. I kept hearing that sound but I couldn't see what was causing it. Then my sharp cowdog eyes picked up some movement.

At first glance it appeared to be a medium sized, bushy-tailed dog stumbling around without a head. Well, that didn't make sense. I'm not so easily fooled. My years of security work told me that there was more to this thing, so I decided to investigate.

A dog without a head? I didn't believe it.

I moved closer and pieced together the following details:

1) The subject wasn't a dog. He was a coyote, age approximately three years and five months, weight thirty-seven pounds, length (including tail) forty-three inches.

2) He was not a he. He was a *she*, meaning a female of the species, rather homely, as coyotes tend to be, but not without charm.

3) Subject had stuck her head into a Hawaiian Punch can with the top cut out. The can had lodged around her ears and gotten stuck there, leaving her blind and helpless.

One of the first rules you learn as a cowdog is that cowdogs and coyotes don't mix. They're natural enemies, the former devoted to the protection of home, livestock, and civilization, the latter devoted to a dissolute style of life based on raiding, depredation, and uncivilized forms of behavior.

In other words, I had every reason to walk away and leave the coyote to her fate—a slow, lingering death. In this business you can't be sentimental.

Still, death inside a Hawaiian Punch can seemed too cruel even for a coyote. I just couldn't walk away and leave her to die, even though I had a feeling that if I helped her, I would regret it.

"Afternoon, ma'am. My name's Hank the Cowdog. Appears to me that you're in distress."

When she heard my voice, she bristled and tried to run away. Didn't go far, though, ran into a rock. She stopped, lay flat on the ground, and didn't move.

I recognized this as the natural sneaky reaction of the coyote breed. When you catch them red-handed, if they can't run away, they'll lie flat on the ground. I suppose they think they're blending into the surroundings. It's hard to say what they think. Coyotes are different.

"You don't need to be afraid, ma'am. I'm here to help you." She didn't say a word or move a muscle. "Lie still and I'll see if I can get that thing off your head."

I don't know how much of this she understood. Coyotes don't speak the same language as dogs, don't you see. Some of the words are similar and some aren't. Modern Doglish and the coyote dialect both come from the same linguistic root, which was the ancient language spoken by our common ancestors many years ago before the species split into *Dogus Domesticus* and *Dogus Coyotus*.

This is pretty technical stuff, and I don't want to bore anyone, but it's important that the reader understand these things.

Well, it just so happened that I was fluent in the coyote dialect, so I decided to address the lady in her own language.

"Me not hurt Missy Coyote. Me friend, me help Missy. Missy have trouble."

"You not hurt?" Her voice echoed inside the can.

"Me not hurt. Me help. Missy Coyote lie still, not move. Hank fixy real quick."

For a long time she didn't speak. Then, "Missy lie still."

It was important that I got the point across to her that I was a friend, don't you see, because it would have been typical coyote behavior for her to jump up, once I got the can off her head, and tear off one of my ears. They're just a little bit crazy, them coyotes, and you've got to be careful.

Anyway, she lay still while I hooked my front paws around the can and started pulling. I pulled and I tugged and I strained and I grunted, and finally the can popped free.

That's when I got my first look at Missy Coyote's face.

I'm not one to gush or be overwhelmed. Let's get that straight right here. My years in the security business have trained me to look upon most things as mere facts, facts to be gathered and studied and analyzed.

I mean, I'd seen women before, lots of 'em, scads of 'em. I'd been through times in my life when women were hanging all over me, and I literally couldn't take a step without bumping into an adoring female.

If you're a cowdog, you get used to this. It's common knowledge that cowdogs are just a little bit special. Read your dog books, ask anyone who knows about dogs, check it out with the experts. They'll tell you that women flip over cowdogs.

What I'm saying—and I'm just trying to put it all into perspective, don't you see—is that I wasn't one of these dogs that chased women all the time or even had much interest in them.

But you know what? When I seen Missy Coyote's face, with those big eyes and that fine tapered nose, I got weak in the legs and kind of swimmy in the head. She was the by George prettiest thang I'd ever laid eyes on.

"Missy Coyote . . . pretty."

She was still blinking her eyes against the glare of the sun. Guess she'd been in that can for a day or two. When she got used to the sunlight, she looked me over real close. Then she smiled.

I melted. I mean, I actually fell over and started kicking my legs in the air. It was an unconscious, unwanted response, not the kind of reaction you'd expect from a professional cowdog. But as I've pointed out before, I was only flesh and blood.

Missy didn't understand my spasm, I reckon, and she came over. Had her head cocked to the side like this—oh well, you can't see—she had her head cocked to the side.

"What wrong? You sick?"

"Yeah, I'm sick all right. I need to get out of here." I struggled to my feet and tried to leave, but my back legs didn't function.

"Not leave," she said. "Stay. Tell name."

I was sure she could hear my heart beating. I could. It was about to take off the top of my head, to be exact. "Me Hank," I finally managed to say.

Her eyes brightened. "Pretty name, Hunk."

"Not Hunk. *Hank*."

She nodded. "Yes, Hunk. Pretty name. Me like. Hunk."

"Whatever you say."

"Me called Girl-Who-Drink-Blood."

"Girl-Who-Drink-Blood!"

She nodded and smiled. "You like?"

There wasn't a whole lot of poetry in that name, seemed to me. Her old lady, or whoever named her, must have been a real barbarian.

"Me no like. Me call you Missy Coyote. Like Missy Coyote moreso. Bloody name not pretty."

She laughed. "Bloody name pretty to coyote. Coyote like blood. Make grow strong, keep hair pretty in winter. Hunk no like blood in winter?"

"Hank eat Co-op dog food in winter, no need blood."

"What means, Co-op dog food?"

"No can explain. Too complicated."

"Why Hunk here, not at people-place with many building and house with chicken?"

"Hank get mad at people, quit job. People no

understand. Hank no more guard chicken. Hank follow outlaw trail."

Her eyes widened. "Outlaw trail dangerous. Live out in wild, coyote around. Coyote not like Hunk."

I decided it was time to turn on some of my charm, just a little at a time. Didn't want to give the girl the full load all at once. "Missy Coyote like Hank?"

She smiled. Mercy! Made me weak in the legs again. "Missy think Hunk cute."

"Ah heck, really? Me cute?"

Her smile faded. "But other coyote not think so. Missy have brother named Scraunch. Not like ranch dog, hurt if find."

"*You're* Scraunch's sister?"

She nodded. I knew about Scraunch, the most notorious outlaw coyote in the whole country. He was big, mean, and utterly heartless. He'd probably killed more chickens and barn cats than any three coyotes on the ranch, and it was common knowledge that he'd kill a stray dog just for the sport of it.

As a matter of fact, me and Scraunch had met on the field of battle and had fought to a draw—which I had considered a victory. That was back in the winter. January, as I recall, yes it was, because we fought in the snow. Scraunch was a real thug.

"How can a nice girl like you have such a bad brother?

She shook her head. "Hunk be careful, maybe go back ranch. Not safe here."

I leaned forward and nuzzled her under the chin with the end of my nose. "I ain't scared. Hank ready to fight whole family for Missy."

I noticed that she started trembling, thought maybe it was the result of my charm. Then she whispered, "Hunk in trouble. Whole family here."

"Huh?"

I looked around. She wasn't kidding. The whole danged family had arrived. We was surrounded by lean-limbed, long-haired, scruffy-tailed, yellow-eyed, slack-jawed, hungry-looking coyotes.

I was in trouble, fellers, and had a feeling that a wreck was coming.

CHAPTER EIGHT

Hank Runs
a Bluff

Missy's old man was the chief. His full proper name was Many-Rabbit-Gut-Eat-in-Full-Moon, which in coyote culture was regarded as a beautiful name. Can you imagine a mother saddling an innocent pup with a name like that? Shows just how backward them coyotes were.

Anyway, nobody used his full name except at rituals and war councils and such. Mostly they called him Chief Gut or just plain Gut.

Gut was an old devil, skinny. You could count every rib he owned on both sides. Looked like a one-way plow with a wet blanket throwed over the discs. Walked with a limp, packed his right front leg which was missing a couple of toes. Had a long scar down the front of his face, nose was all beat up, and his left ear looked as though the rats had been chewing on it.

He came limping over to where I was and, strangely enough, he had a smile on his face. Made me feel a little better about things.

"Ah ha," he laughed, "daughter catch dog! Coyote girl pretty, huh?"

"Mighty pretty, yes she is."

"You like, huh?" He turned to the other coyotes. "Dog like Girl-Who-Drink-Blood. Think she pretty." They roared at that, got a good chuckle out of it. I must have missed the joke. Old Gut turned back to me. "Oh foolish dog to chase coyote girl into canyon. Berry berry foolish you leave ranch, come here without big-hat and boom-boom."

I'm doing my best to translate this conversation from the coyote dialect, but maybe I ought to pause here to clear up some of the terminology.

Big-hat was the coyote word for cowboy, and *boom-boom* meant gun. Thought I better get that straight. I mean, you can't expect everyone to be fluent in three or four or five languages. I was, but that was just part of my job, one of the many things a top-notch cowdog had to master before he could take over a ranch and run it the way it ought to be run.

I might also mention that I had a fair knowledge of the coon, possum, and badger dialects, and I could bluff my way through in chicken and prairie dog. Actually, chicken is pretty simple. Chickens are so dumb that they only have about half a dozen words in the whole language, and three of those words are just different ways of saying *help*!

All right, we've got that out of the way. Now, where was I? Old Gut turned to me. "Oh foolish dog to chase coyote girl into canyon. Berry..." We've already heard that. "Now you in big trouble, ha! You do good job, Daughter, catch dog."

"Not catch dog," she said. "Dog help, save life. Name Hunk. Hunk friend."

The old man scowled. "Hunk not friend. Fight coyote many time away from chicken. He chicken dog."

Chicken dog. Them was fightin' words. If Missy hadn't been there to hold me back, I might have cleaned house on the whole coyote nation. Me and old man Gut went nose to nose and were growling at each other when I caught some motion out of the corner of my eye. I looked. It was Scraunch.

He was crouched low, walking real slow. Hair along his backbone was bristled all the way from the back of his neck to the tip of his tail. Had a

snarl on his mouth that showed two rows of long white fangs. He was a big dude, tall, brawny, raw-boned, and so ugly that a guy could hardly stand to look him in the face. Kind of throwed a chill in me.

Old man Gut backed off. "Now what you say, Chicken Dog? You scared betcha, huh?"

I swallered and tried to keep my knees from going out on me. "Naw, I ain't scared."

"You not scared Scraunch, you not smart. Scraunch berry bad fellow."

I glanced at Missy. "Tell your brother that I don't like the look on his face."

She told him. He stopped and a roar of laughter went up from the other coyotes. When they quit yipping and howling, I went on. "Tell your brother that if he takes one more step, I'm gonna use him to sweep this whole pasture, and when I get done, there won't be a cactus bush left in Ochiltree County."

She told him. He grinned and took another step.

"Tell your brother that I saw that, and I won't forget it."

Missy shook her head. "Not talk so big. Make Scraunch mad. Big mouth make big trouble."

One of the first rules you learn in security work is an old piece of dog wisdom: never bite if you can bark; never bark if you can growl; never growl if you can talk; and never talk if you can run.

In other words, when the odds are against you, the best kind of fight is none at all. That was my strategy, see. The longer I talked, the longer I could stay alive. And who knows, I just might say something that would change Scraunch's mind about tearing me limb from limb, though I didn't have a great deal of hope.

He was standing maybe four, five feet in front

of me. A hush had fallen over the tribe and all eyes were on the two of us. He sat down and leered at me. And I mean leered, brother. That wasn't no ordinary grin.

I leered right back, tried to anyway, though I'd never really perfected a good leer. Then I turned to Missy again.

"Tell your brother that I've changed my mind. If he can mind his manners and act right, we'll forget the whole thing."

Missy started to speak, but Scraunch lifted his paw for silence. "Not speak through sister," he said in a deep rumbling voice. "You have talk, you speak Scraunch."

"All right," I nodded, "you asked for it, you've really done it this time. I was prepared to forget the whole thing and just let it slide, but by George if you're going to keep pushing and mouthing off, well hey, this could get serious. Come on."

He didn't move.

"*Come on!* Get off your duff and let's settle this thing once and for all. I'm tired of waiting. I mean, I came out here to get *you*, Scraunch. Oh, I know, you thought I was messing around with your sister. Ha! That's just what I wanted you to think. It was a trap, Scraunch, and you walked right into it.

"Oh, what a dumb brute you are! I didn't

think you'd actually fall for it. I never dreamed it would be this easy. All these months I've been waiting to even the score between us, and I never dreamed I could just walk into the canyon and you'd come to me!"

Speaking of silence, them coyotes was silent. Guess they couldn't believe what they were hearing. Scraunch glanced at Chief Gut and Gut glanced at Missy and Missy glanced at me, and I gave her a smile and a wink.

Scraunch stood up, and so did the hair on the back of his neck. "Scraunch kill chicken dog."

"You think so? *You actually think that?*" I cut loose with a wild laugh. "Holy cats, where have you been all your life? You've been up in the bojacks too long, Scraunch, you're so country it hurts. I mean, you're pathetic. I almost feel sorry for you." I took a step toward him. "You still don't understand, do you? It still hasn't soaked through your thick barbarian skull that you've walked right into my trap. Ho, I can't believe this!"

Scraunch cut his eyes toward old Gut.

"Scraunch kill chicken dog." But there was a little less conviction this time.

"Okay." I marched right up to him, until there weren't more than a couple of inches between our noses. "If you're bound and determined to go through with this, let's get it on. But first, I want you to do something. I want you to ask yourself this question: Why would a smart dog walk right into the middle of a bunch of coyotes, in *their* country? Put your little brain to work on that, Scraunch. If you figger it out, you'll know the secret. I'll give you thirty seconds."

Nobody moved. There wasn't a sound, not a whisper. Fifteen seconds went by *real* slow. I was in the process of checking out the escape routes when an old woman coyote (Scraunch's mother, it turned out) broke the circle and came out to him. She whispered something in his ear.

"No!" he growled. "Scraunch not scared, kill chicken dog!"

The old lady went to whispering again, then old Chief Gut limped over and joined the conference. It was kind of agitated. They growled and snapped and snarled—typical coyote family discussion, I would imagine.

"All right," I yelled, "time's up. I'm out of patience. Have you figgered out the secret or shall we start spilling blood?"

The old lady led Scraunch away. He glared daggers at me over his shoulder. Old Chief Gut came over and stood in front of me.

"Not fight today."

"Rats," I said, and almost fainted with relief. "All right, if that's the way you want it. We'll let it slide this time, but I'm warning you, don't ever let this happen again."

"Not happen again."

"Good. I guess we understand each other."

"We understand."

"Very good. Now, if you coyotes will just stay where you are, I'll slip out of here and get on my way." I started backing away and ran into three big coyote bucks. "'Scuse me, boys, if you'll just..."

"Hunk not understand." Missy came over. "Hunk stay, become coyote warrior, prove himself many fight and marry Missy Coyote."

"*HUH?*"

I shot a glance at Chief Gut, who was grinning and bobbing his head. "Yes, berry good you stay. Make outlaw, make warrior."

"Make warrior? Well, I...I've always wanted...but I really have to..." I tried to ease around the three coyotes who were blocking my path. When I moved, they moved. They didn't intend to let me out of there, is the way it looked.

"Stay, not leave," the chief went on. "Old coyote tradition, adopt brave dog, make brother."

"Brave? Well, I can set you straight on that. You see..."

"Together we kill many chicken, eat cat every day, howl at moon, oh boy."

"I don't know about eating cat. I never..." I tried again to edge around those three bruisers, but they pushed me back.

"*Dog not leave,*" said the chief.

"Yes sir."

"Maybe later marry daughter, have many pup. Everybody happy but Scraunch. Too bad. He not understand secret."

There was no chance of me getting out of there, so I walked over to the chief. "You figgered out the secret?"

He laughed and nodded his head. "Oh yes, berry much."

"What did you figger out?"

Gut glanced over his shoulders and brought his mouth right next to my ear. "Secret too secret to tell."

"You got it, all right, you sure did."

We had a good laugh, me and Old Gut, but I doubt that we were laughing about the same thing.

CHAPTER NINE

Me Just a Worthless Coyote

That business about the secret was the perfect stroke, and it probably saved my life. In desperation, I had lucked into it. Turns out that coyotes are superstitious animals, even though they're known to be cunning and vijalent vijalunt vijallunt vijjullunt . . .

I don't know how to spell that word. Spelling is a pain in the neck. I do my best with it, but I figger if a guy has tremendous gifts as a writer, his audience will forgive a few slip-ups in the spelling department.

I mean, it doesn't take any brains to open a dickshunary and look up a word. Anybody can do that. The real test of a writer comes in the creative process. I try to attend to the big picture, don't you see, and let the spelling take care of itself.

Vidgalent. Vidgallunt. Still doesn't look right.

Anyway, coyotes are superstitious brutes, and that deal about the secret caught them just right and saved my hide. Actually, it did better than that. It made me a kind of celebrity in the tribe, and I was treated like a visiting dignutarry digneterry dignitary, who cares?

By everyone but Scraunch, that is, and he continued to give me hateful glances and mutter under his breath every time our paths crossed. I couldn't blame him for being sore. I had won and he had lost, and you can't expect everyone to be a good loser. As we say in the security business, show me a good loser and I'll show you a loser.

Scraunch had lost a big one, and I was confident that he would hate my guts forevermore, even though there was a good chance that I would eventually become his brother-in-law.

You know, when Missy had first mentioned that possibility, it hadn't struck me as a real good idea. I suppose at that time I was still thinking of going back home, back to Drover and Pete, the chickens, the sewer, the cowboys, my old job. But a couple of days in the coyote village pretty muchly convinced me that I had found my true place in the world as a savage.

The life of a savage ain't too bad. I admit that I was raised with a natural ~~prejjudise~~ ~~predguduss~~ *bias* against coyotes. Ma always told us that they were lazy, sneaky, undisciplined, and didn't have any ambition. But what chapped her most about coyotes was that they ate rotten meat and it made them smell bad.

True, every word of it. But what she *didn't* tell us was that laziness and riotous living can be a lot of fun. I don't blame her for not telling us that. I mean, she was trying to raise a litter of registered, papered, blue-ribbon, top-of-the-line cowdogs, and there's no better way to mess up a good cowdog than to let him discover that goofing off beats the heck out of hard work.

I discovered it by accident, and once I had a taste of indolence, I loved it. I mean, all at once I had no responsibilities, no cares, no worries. When I woke up in the morning, I didn't have to wonder if my ranch had made it through another night, or if I would get yelled at again for something I hadn't done.

About a week after I joined the tribe, I made friends with two brothers named Rip and Snort. They were what you'd call typical good-old-boy coyotes: filthy, smelled awful, not real smart, loved to fight and have a good time, and had no more ambition than a couple of fence posts.

If Rip and Snort took a shine to you, you had two of the best friends in the world. If they didn't happen to like your looks or your attitude, you were in a world of trouble. I got along with them.

One evening along toward sunset, they came around and asked if I wanted to go carousing. I was feeling refreshed, since I'd slept a good part of the day—got up around noon and ate a piece of a rabbit that Missy had caught, then went back to bed. I was all rested up and said, "Sure I'd love to go carousing."

So off we went, me and Rip and Snort, on a big adventure. We went down the canyon, crossed that big sandy draw that cuts through there, then on across some rolling country until we came to an old silage pit. I'd been by it many times, but I'd never taken the time to go into the pit and check things out. By the time I took over the ranch, the cowboys had quit feeding silage, so I didn't know much about it.

One of the things I didn't know about silage was that it's fermented, which means that it's got some alkyhall in it, which means that if a guy eats enough of it, his attitude about the world will begin to change.

All those years I'd spent on the ranch, and I

never knew any of that. But Rip and Snort knew all about silage, yes they did, and they had made a well-packed trail into and out of the silage pit.

So we started eating silage. Struck me as kind of bitter at first, but the more I ate the less I noticed the bitterness. By George, after about an hour of that, I thought it was as sweet as honey.

Well, we ate and we laughed and we laughed and we ate, and when it came time to leave, Rip and Snort had to drag me out of there, fellers, 'cause I just couldn't get enough of that fine stuff.

A big moon was out and we went single file down a cow path, Snort in the lead, me in the middle, and Rip on the caboose. Funny thing, that cow path kept wiggling around and I had a devil of a time trying to stay on it. I asked Rip about it and he said he was having the same trouble, derned path kept jumping from side to side. (I suspect the silage had something to do with it, is what I suspect.)

Well, next thing I knew, Snort topped a rise and came to a sudden halt, which caused a little pile-up, with me running into Snort and Rip running into me because couldn't any of us see real well at that point.

"Stop here," said Snort, "sing many song. Sing pretty, sing loud, teach Hunk coyote song."

So we all sat down on our haunches, throwed back our heads, and started singing. Let's see if I can remember how that song went.

"Me just a worthless coyote, me howling
    at the moon.
Me like to sing and holler, me crazy as a
    loon.
Me not want job or duties, no church or
    Sunday school.
Me just a worthless coyote . . ." and I don't
    remember the last part, only it rhymed
    with "school." Pool or drool, something
    like that.

It was a crackerjack of a song. We ripped through it a couple of times, until I had her down. Then we divided up. Snort took the bass, Rip carried the melody, and I got up on the high tenor.

Don't know as I ever heard better singing. It was one of them priceless moments in life when three very gifted guys come together and blend their talents and sort of raise the cultural standards of the whole danged world. I mean, it was that good.

We sang it four or five times, then all at once Snort's ears perked up and he lifted his paw. We stopped and listened. Off in the distance, we heard yapping. There was something familiar about that yap, but for a minute I couldn't place it. Then it occurred to me that we were sitting on a spot just a quarter mile north of ranch headquarters.

That yapping was coming from Drover.

I think Rip and Snort had took a notion to amble on down there and see if they could get into a fight. I had to explain that they couldn't run fast enough to get Drover into a fight, that it would be a waste of their time.

"Let me go down and talk to him," I said. "He's an old buddy of mine. We used to work together. Maybe he'll come back and sing with us. We could use another guy on baritone."

They shrugged. Snort sat down and started scratching his ear. "More fun fight, but singing okay too. We wait."

So I trotted down to the ranch, weaving a little bit from side to side and humming "Me just a Worthless Coyote." Say, that was a good song!

When I was, oh, twenty, twenty-five yards away, I slowed to a walk. I could see Drover up ahead of me. He was peering off in the distance. The little dope hadn't even seen me. I decided to stop and watch him for a minute.

He was all bunched up and tense. Off in the distance he could hear Rip and Snort laughing and belching and having a good time. He'd cock his head and listen for a minute, then he'd give out a yip-yip-yip. On every yip, all four feet went off the ground. Then he'd stop and listen again.

He never saw me, never had the slightest notion that I was sitting ten yards away from him, watching the whole show. This was my replacement, understand, the guy who had taken over my job as Head of Ranch Security. I didn't need anyone to tell me that the ranch had gone completely and absolutely to pot.

I cleared my throat. Drover froze. "What was that? Who's there?"

"What's going on, son?"

He gave out his usual squeak and in a flash he was high-balling it for the machine shed, squalling like a turpentined cat. He'd gone maybe ten, twelve yards when he slowed to a walk, then stopped.

"Hank, is that you?"

"Uh-huh."

"It is?"

"Uh-huh."

"How can I be sure? I thought you'd left the country."

"Well, why don't you just trot your little self over here and see."

He came real slow, a few steps at a time. "It . . . it sure sounds like you."

"Son of a gun."

"You're not fooling me, are you, Hank?"

"Get over here and quit messing around."

"Okay, okay, I just . . . I want to be sure, that's all." He came creeping up to me. "Hank?"

"Boo."

He screamed and jumped straight up into the air. "Hank, stop that, don't do that to me! My nerves . . ."

"Drover, you ought to be ashamed of yourself. What a pitiful excuse you are for a night watchman. I could have carried off half the chickenhouse and you never would have gotten the news."

He hung his head. "I know it. I'm a failure. Every morning I wake up and say, 'Here's another day for you to mess up, Drover.' And I do, every one of them. It hasn't been the same since you left, Hank."

"I knew it wouldn't. I tried to tell 'em but they wouldn't listen. I mean, you can't treat a good dog like a dog and expect to keep him."

"Gosh, I wish you'd come back."

I laughed. "You can forget that, son, cause it'll

never happen. I've found a better life."

He looked me over real careful. "What's come over you, Hank? You look different. You smell different. You stink."

"I've joined the coyote tribe."

I heard him gasp. "No!"

"That's right, and if you had a brain in your head, you'd come along and join up with 'em too. It ain't a bad life, let me tell you."

He took a couple of steps back. "I can't believe it. What would your mother say?"

"She'd say I was a turncoat and a traitor. So what? I tried the straight life, I did my job, and what did I get? Abuse. Ingratitude. No thanks, life's too short for that. I'll cast my lot with the outlaws of the world."

"Three weeks ago," he said in a quavery voice, "you were on the side of law and order, trying to catch the murderers. Now you're one of them."

"That's right."

He started crying. "Oh Hank, I can't take this! I used to admire you so much. You were my hero, I thought you were the greatest dog in the world. Since I was a pup, I just wanted to be like you, brave and strong and fearless . . ."

"Knock it off, Drover, I don't want to hear that stuff."

"...and dedicated to duty. I knew I could never be as good as you, but I wanted to try. You were my idol, Hank."

"Cut it out, would you?"

"Come back home, Hankie. I need you. The ranch needs you. We all need you."

That kind of struck me in the heart, hearing Drover say those things. Then Rip and Snort called for me.

"Hunk! Come, sing. We tired wait!"

"Who's that?" Drover whispered.

"Oh, some of my pals. Come on up the hill with me, Drover, and I'll show you a good time, introduce you to my friends."

"Are they *drunk* like you?"

There was a little edge in his voice. He'd never talked to me like that before. "Well uh, maybe they are and maybe they ain't. Who cares?"

"I care. I don't associate with coyote trash."

"Well, lah-tee-dah! Aren't we high and mighty tonight."

Drover dried his eyes with the back of his paw. "I better get on back to the ranch. I'm on guard tonight."

I laughed in his face. "You're on guard! Son, you're a sorry excuse for a guard dog, running for the machine shed every time you hear a sound."

"I'm not going to run anymore, Hank. Somebody's got to protect the ranch. We can't depend on you anymore."

"You'll run. You always have, you always will."

"I ain't going to run."

"Sure you will, and I can prove it. *BOO!*" He didn't run. "That don't prove a thing. When the time comes, when the chips are down, you'll run and hide."

He looked me in the eye. "No I won't. And Hank, if you come with them, I won't run from you either." He turned and started walking away.

"You always were a little chump."

He stopped. "I may be a chump, Hank, but I'm not a traitor. Good-bye."

"Go on, you little dummy, who needs you anyway! Sawed-off, stub-tailed, self-righteous little pipsqueak!"

Drover went his way and I went mine. On my way up the hill, I could hear the boys singing "Me just a Worthless Coyote" again. I took my place between Rip and Snort and started belting out the high tenor. We went on like that all night long, singing and laughing and chasing mice.

But it wasn't quite as much fun this time.

CHAPTER TEN

Aged Mutton

Must have been a couple of days later that I was sitting on the edge of the caprock, sunning myself and looking off in the distance. I'd been there most of the day, thinking about things and enjoying the quiet.

The coyote village was awful noisy. Seemed that somebody was always in the midst of a squabble. When a husband and wife had a difference of opinion, they just by George had a knock-down drag-out fight, right there in front of everybody. Nobody ever seemed to get hurt in these brawls, and I guess they managed to solve their problems, but I could never get used to the noise of it.

And the hair. After one of them family fights,

the air was full of fur. A guy could hardly breathe for the hair.

And then there was the kids. There must have been ten or twelve pups in the village, and let me tell you about coyote pups.

Now, a *dog* pup is kind of cute. I'm not real fond of babies, understand, but even I have to admit that a little old cowdog pup is pretty cute. He'll be fat as a butterball and covered with silky hair, and when he looks up at you with those big soft eyes, you can't help but smile and say, "How's it going, kid?"

Coyote pups ain't cute. They look mean, they sound mean, they act mean, and fellers, they *are* mean. They've got two jaws full of teeth that are as sharp as needles, and their idea of good clean fun is to slip up behind some unsuspecting somebody (me, for instance) and just bite the heck out of his tail.

As a rule, I'm a pretty good sport. I was a kid once myself and I got into my share of mischief, but I can't get used to people biting my tail. I mean, there's something kind of special and private about a guy's tail. If he's got any pride at all, he tries to keep it nice, and he's a little fussy about scabs and bald spots and tooth marks and slobber and all that stuff.

What I'm saying is that my tail ain't a play toy.

But these kids, they'd sneak up behind me and sink their little needle teeth into my tail. First few times, I just growled at 'em: "Here! Y'all go on, get out of here!" Didn't work. Coyotes are a little slow about taking a hint.

They came back and did it again, so I took sterner measures—cuffed one of 'em. Know what he did then? He *bit* me on the paw. Well, I wasn't going to take that off a dern kid, so I bit him on the scruff of the neck, and he somehow worked his way around and got hold of my left ear.

That got me all inflamed, don't you see, and I put the boy on the ground and was spanking some manners into him when his momma walked up.

"*You brute*, leave my junior alone!"

"Huh?"

I looked around just in time to get slapped across the mouth. "There, bully!"

I suppose I shouldn't have slapped her back. But I did. *Whop*, right across the nose. "Maybe you can teach that boy some manners."

Whop! "Chicken dog!"

Whop! "Wild hag!"

She burst into tears and went bawling to her husband saying I was just an animal and had beat up her danged kid and called her a wild hag. Turned out she was Scraunch's woman, and here he came, all humped up and hair raised and yellow eyes aflaming.

I had taken about all I wanted off Scraunch and his family, and I was ready to go into combat, but Missy and her father jumped in between us and averted a civil war.

But the incident didn't do much to improve relations between me and Missy's brother. I had a feeling that sooner or later we were going to have a showdown.

Funny thing about all this. Them coyotes didn't mind chewing on each other. I mean, they were fighting all the time. But when I tried it, they didn't like it. Made me think that no matter how long I stayed there, they would always think of me as an outsider.

Anyway, I was sitting on the ledge, off to myself and away from the noise, when Missy came up behind me. She nuzzled me with her nose and ran her claws down my backbone. She knew I liked that.

"Something wrong? Hunk look sad."

"Oh, it's nothing. Just wanted to be alone, I guess."

"Not enjoy other coyote?"

"Well . . . do you ever get tired of all the noise, all that fighting and yelling?"

She shook her head. "That happy sound. When coyote happy, make bunch noise. When we married, we happy, make bunch noise too."

"I see, yes, well, I guess we have that to look forward to, don't we?"

"When pup come, even more noise, oh boy."

"Oh boy."

"Hunk not be sad. Missy have something make Hunk feel good. We have feast, special food just for Hunk."

I followed her into the village. We went to her parents' den. They were sitting out in front and the old lady was pulling cockleburs out of the chief's tail. Missy asked her mother if she would prepare a special meal, just for me. She said she would. She left and was gone for ten, fifteen minutes.

I tried to make conversation with the old man but it wasn't easy. He started talking about the old days, about a time when he went a couple of rounds with a skunk. He seemed to think this story was hilarious. I thought it was moderately funny.

The chief was still cackling at his own wonderful story when the old lady returned, dragging in some horrible stinking something or other.

I turned to Missy. "What's that?"

"Aged mutton."

"Aged mutton?"

She nodded and smiled. "Special feast make Hunk forget sadness."

Aged mutton. No doubt it had been buried for a while. It was green, dotted here and there with white spots which turned out to be maggots. The smell alone could have taken the paint off a corral fence. The taste of such rot was too horrible to imagine.

The old lady dragged it up and dropped it right at my feet. When she smiled at me, she looked an awful lot like her daughter, except she had several teeth missing and some of that green stuff hanging from her lower lip.

"Meat age for many month, just right for Hunk now."

The old man threw back his head, let out a howl, and dived into it. The old lady did the same. Missy did the same. I took a deep breath, said a little prayer, and dove in too.

Let's don't go into any details. It was bad. It was so bad that there are no words to describe it. I'll say no more.

An hour later, I was lying down, with my head over a cliff. I had emptied my body of everything

but blood and a few bones. Missy stood over me, stroking my brow. She had been very nice about it. They all had been, even my future mother-in-law. She had decided that I had drunk some brackish water and that's what had made me sick.

"Hunk feel better now?"

"Feel better, sort of."

"Hunk like coyote feast, oh boy?"

"Oh boy."

"Now Hunk make ready for big raid?"

I raised up my head. "Huh?"

That was the first I had heard about the raid. This was going to be my big chance to prove to Missy's ma and pa that I was worthy of their daughter.

Scraunch was putting the deal together, a raid on the ranch.

The Attack on the Ranch

A long about dark the coyote village came to life. Everybody was excited.

"Fresh chicken, fresh cat!" they shouted. "Oh boy!"

Even the kids were excited. They chased each other around, practiced howling, and played a game called "Get the Dog." The idea of the game was that two kids played coyotes and one played the guard dog. The coyotes lured the dog out into a fight and then jumped him.

I had played that game myself, only when I'd played it it hadn't been a game, and I'd been on the dog side. I'd never thought it was much fun either.

After the sun went down, Scraunch climbed up on a pile of rocks and gave a speech to the whole village. He was a firebrand and a rubble-rouser, and he preached the kind of hot gospel them coyotes wanted to hear.

"Jackrabbit run too fast, make coyote tired to catch. Mouse run down hole, coyote have to dig, make tired too. But *chicken* . . . chicken easy! Chicken nice and fat, sit on nest, not fight. Chicken plump and juicy. This night, everybody eat chicken!"

A cheer went up from the crowd. I was standing beside Missy, and she whooped and hollered along with the rest of them.

Scraunch waited for the cheering to die down and glanced over at me. "Ranch not have big guard dog now, only little white dog with cut-off tail. Maybe this night we kill dog too."

Another cheer went up. Scraunch watched me with a half-smile on his face. When I didn't cheer with the rest of them, he said, "What you say, Hunk? Maybe you help kill little white dog, huh?"

"Maybe so, Scraunch, maybe so."

Then he led the crowd in singing, "Me just a Worthless Coyote," which was everybody's favorite song and sort of the coyote national anthem. I noticed that it brought tears to old Chief Gut's eyes. Guess it brought back memories of his younger days.

When the song started, Rip and Snort came over to where I was and wanted to harmonize, just the way we did the night we went carousing. I tried but didn't feel much like singing.

But Rip and Snort bellered and howled and had themselves a big time. They were all excited about the raid, and they got into an argument over which one was going to give Drover the worst whipping. Listening to them snarl at each other, I got a funny feeling about good old boys. They have a way of changing into *mean* old boys and pretty quick.

The singing stopped and it was time to start the raid. Scraunch led the whole village in a howl, then those of us who were going on the raid lined up in a single file. Missy came over to tell me good-bye.

"Hunk have good fight, bring back fat chicken, prove to everybody that he good coyote."

"Thanks, Missy, I'll do my best."

"Then we marry, have seven-eight little pup."

"Seven or eight?"

She gave a yip and a howl. "Maybe nine-ten, oh boy!"

She nuzzled me under the chin, stepped back, and gave me a smile. Geeze, she had a pretty face, but you know what? When she smiled, I saw her mother's face and remembered that aged mutton. It derned near ruined the occasion for me.

Scraunch came down the line, checking things out and giving orders to the men. When he came to me, he gave me a hard look.

"Better not make mistake. Scraunch watch close."

"You do that, Scraunch. You might learn something."

He gave me a sneer and went back to the front. With the rest of the village cheering, we marched down the canyon rim in a trot.

Once we left the village, Scraunch passed the order for silence. Down in the valley we got on a cow trail and followed it south toward the creek.

I couldn't help wondering where Drover was and what he was doing right now. Had he heard the singing? Did he run to the machine shed or was he out on patrol? I hoped, for his sake, that he was in the backest corner of the shed, 'cause these coyotes were in a dangerous mood.

As we slipped along through the night, I started putting a few things together. It was pretty clear by this time that Scraunch was the one who had been responsible for the chicken murders. He'd been slipping down there by himself and killing one or two a night, and now he'd decided to launch a full-scale invasion and share the spoils of war with the rest of the coyotes.

Funny, I'd solved the case, only now I was working for the other side. Life sure does play tricks on a guy, makes it awful hard to plan for the future. Growing up, I never would have dreamed that I'd end up a chicken-killer. I was kind of glad Ma wasn't around to see it.

About two hundred yards north of the ranch, Scraunch called a halt and gave the final orders for the attack. He told Rip and Snort to circle around and come in from the south, and sent another couple of guys over to the west.

He hadn't given me any orders, and that was good. I figgered I could lay low, stay out of the way, and show up when all the dust cleared.

"*You.*"

I looked around. "Huh?"

"You go with Scraunch. We get little white dog. Find out how bad you want sister."

"Well uh, surely I don't deserve such an honor."

"Not talk, only fight."

The others left, and me and Scraunch started sneaking toward the ranch. I felt sick. Things had gotten out of control. I hadn't wanted it to happen this way, me against my old buddy Drover. In his own bungling way, Drover was a nice dog. We'd had our squabbles and differences, but we'd had some good times too.

About twenty-five yards out, Scraunch stopped and dropped down into the grass. I squinted into the darkness and saw Drover standing beside the northeast corner of the machine shed. Just as you might expect, he wasn't looking in our direction. The little runt had no idea what was fixing to break loose.

A laugh growled in Scraunch's throat. "This easy. Dog stupid."

I couldn't argue with him. Facts is facts.

We crawled forward another ten, fifteen yards. Then, off to the south, Rip and Snort raised a howl. Drover jumped up in the air and faced the south. I could see that he was shivering. Then the boys off to the west raised a howl, and Drover faced *that* direction.

Scraunch growled and Drover faced us. His head was cocked sideways and one ear stood up. That meant he still didn't see us.

But he was beginning to get the picture. The ranch was surrounded. I kept waiting for him to run, but he didn't.

Scraunch pushed himself up out of the grass. "You go first. I watch."

"Who me? Well uh, seems to me that . . ."

The hair went up on the back of his neck and there was murder in those yellow eyes. "You go first or I cut throat right here!"

I could tell he wasn't kidding. "I just thought . . . there's no need to . . . I see what you mean, yes, I'll go first."

I stood up. Scraunch threw back his head and let loose the bloodiest howl I ever heard (sent shivers all the way down to the end of my tail, is how frightful it was). He gave me a shove and the attack was on.

Drover heard us coming. He started yipping and jumping up and down, but he stood his ground. I could hear myself talking: "Run, Drover, while there's still time." My voice got louder. "You got no chance, Drover, don't try to be a hero."

Next thing I knew, I was yelling. "Drover, run for the shed! You're outnumbered, they'll kill you, run for your life!"

The little mutt was so scared he was spinning in circles and jumping up and down at the same time. But he still didn't leave his post.

By this time I could see Rip and Snort sneaking up behind him, the moonlight glinting off their teeth and eyes. They didn't look like good old boys any more. They had murder on their minds.

Behind me, Scraunch was screaming, "Kill, kill!"

All at once, something snapped inside my head. I felt wild and crazy. I headed straight for Drover. I'll never forget the look in his eyes. He was more than scared. He was bewildered, didn't know what was happening to him.

He turned to face my charge. As I flew past

him and took aim for Snort, I yelled, "This is it, son, hell against Texas! Fight for your life!"

I caught Snort by surprise and sent him rolling down the hill. That gave me just enough time to catch Rip as he was making a dive for the back of Drover's neck. Hit him in midair and knocked him on his back.

By this time Scraunch had plowed Drover under and was standing on top of him, ready to tear out his throat. I lit right in the middle of his back, got a bite on his right ear, and started chewing.

That took his mind off Drover. He jumped straight up and pitched me off. I got to my feet and he got to his feet, and we faced each other.

"Call off your boys, Scraunch. Let's make it me and you, one on one."

He grinned. "Chicken dog die for this."

I had a little piece of his ear in my mouth, and I spit it out at his feet. Out of the corner of my eye, I saw a light come on in the house. That was my only hope. If High Loper didn't hurry and get his pants on and grab his gun, I was a dead dog.

"Seems you lost a piece of one ear, Scraunch. If you'll come a little closer, I'll work on that other one so's they'll match."

Scraunch cut his eyes toward Rip and Snort. "Get him."

Rip and Snort gave me kind of a mournful look. It was decision time. They had to choose between an old drinkin' buddy and their own flesh and blood.

"Get him!"

They licked their lips and swallered and glanced at each other. And they chose flesh and blood. They started creeping toward me.

"Drover," I said in a low voice, "keep 'em off my back, son, or we're finished."

Drover squeaked. He was too scared to talk.

Rip and Snort and the other two coyotes started closing in on me.

"Hunk stupid dog," said Scraunch. "Stupid dog pay with life."

"You could be right, Scraunch, but you've got it to do."

We was totally surrounded and it was every man for himself. I figgered I might as well leave this old life with another piece of Scraunch's ear, so I made a dive at him.

We collided and went up on our hind legs. I boxed him across the nose and he boxed me right back. Made my eyes water. I clawed his hip and he clawed mine. I went for his ear and he went for mine. We chewed and snapped and snarled and growled.

I think old Scraunch was a little surprised that a cowdog could give him such a tussle.

I was holding my own until they jumped me from behind, two or three of 'em, didn't get a good count, but it was plenty enough to finish me off.

They wrestled me down, throwed me on my back, and pinned me to the ground. Scraunch walked up and straddled me, showing his big, sharp teeth.

"Now you die."

He went for my throat and I heard Saint Peter blow his horn.

CHAPTER TWELVE

The Exciting Conclusion

Saint Peter's horn had an odd kind of sound. Instead of saying, "toot-toot," as you might expect, it said "bal-LOOM!" And it made fire that lit up the sky, and something went whistling over our heads.

Shucks, that wasn't Saint Peter at all. It was High Loper, and he was standing on the back porch, blasting away with his pump shotgun.

Scraunch had just fitted my throat around his jaws and was fixing to remove it when the artillery opened up. He threw his head up in the air.

"Scraunch hurry!" Said one of the other coyotes. "Kill dog fast!"

Scraunch was going for the throat again for a

117

quick kill when the second load of shot arrived. Loper had found his range, and he distributed a full load of number seven birdshot about evenly through the crowd.

You never heard such yipping and squalling. Them coyotes were jumping around like crickets in a shoebox, knocking each other down trying to get out of there.

All but Scraunch. He backed away real slow. "Another time, Hunk. We meet again."

"Yeah, and so's your old man!" That's the best I could do on the spur of the moment and with a sore throat.

I picked myself up and limped around. I had some nicks and cuts but nothing was busted. I'd come through the fight in pretty good shape, all things considered.

Loper came running up the hill, slipping shells into his shotgun. He hadn't taken the time to put on his jeans, God bless him, which probably saved my life. All he had on was a pair of brown and white striped boxer shorts, his cowboy boots, and a tee shirt with three holes in it, and also some windmill grease. Legs looked awful pale and skinny sticking out of them boxer shorts.

"Danged coyotes!" he yelled. Then he looked at me and—this next part is kind of shocking, so prepare yourself—he looked at me and—still gets me a little choked up, even today—he *SMILED*!

That's right, he smiled at *me*, Hank the Cowdog. I mean, I was just by George overwhelmed by it. In my whole career, I couldn't remember Loper ever smiling at me.

"Hank!" he cried. "You've come back home!" He laid down the gun and came over and throwed his arms around me and gave me a big hug. "By golly it's good to have you . . ." I licked him on the face. He drew back and wrinkled his nose. "Dog, you stink! Where have you been?"

Aged mutton, is where I'd been.

About then, Sally May came up the hill, tying the strings on her housecoat and pushing the hair out of her eyes, which were red and puffy. "What is it, what's wrong?"

"Coyotes, hon, a whole pack of 'em. I bet they were trying to get into the chickenhouse, but old Hank suddenly appeared—good dog, Hank, good dog—and he and Drover . . . where's Drover?"

That was a good question. I'd kind of forgot about him in all the excitement. Then Sally May gave a cry. "Oh no! I think he's . . . he's not moving, just lying there."

I've already mentioned that in the security business, you can't afford to let your emotions get the best of you. I mean, it's a tough business and you have to be prepared for the worst.

I considered myself pretty muchly hardboiled, but when I saw little Drover stretched out there on the ground, it really ripped me. I mean, the little guy had done his best to protect the ranch, he'd stood his ground under combat conditions. But now . . .

We all went over to him. He didn't move a muscle, not even a hair, and it was pretty clear to me that he was, well, dead. A big tear came out of my eye and rolled down my nose. I had to turn away, couldn't stand to look anymore.

Loper bent down and there was a long silence. "His heart's beating. He's still alive."

"Thank goodness," said Sally May.

"Actually, I can't see anything wrong with him. He's got a nick on his nose and one ear's been chewed on, but other than that, he looks all right."

"Let's take him to the house. I'll make him a nice little bed and try to get some warm milk down him."

Loper gathered him up in his arms and they started down the hill. I just happened to be looking at Drover when, all at once, one eye popped open. He glanced around and closed it again.

The little runt was half-stepping, is what he was doing, and he wasn't about to miss out on that soft bed and warm milk. All right, maybe he fainted or something in the heat of battle, sounds like something he'd do, but I could see that he wasn't feeling no pain.

It took him two whole days to get over his craving for warm milk and a soft bed, and he probably could have strung it out another day or two, only he peed on the carpet and got throwed out.

I was down by the corrals when he came padding up. "Hi, Hank, what's going on?"

I was working on another case and didn't really want to be disturbed. "Hello, Half-stepper. What's going on is that some of us have to work for a living so that others of us can attend to the milk-drinking."

He shrugged and gave me a silly grin. "I'm feeling much better now, thanks."

"I'll bet."

"What you working on?"

I glanced over both shoulders before I answered. "There's something funny going on around here, Drover. Look at these tracks." I pointed to the tracks but he didn't look.

"Tracks are down here in the dirt, son. That's where you find most tracks, on the ground."

"Hank, tell me something. Did you really join up with the coyotes? I mean, did you really think you could live with them?"

I walked a short distance away and for a minute I didn't answer. "Drover, if I tell you something, will you swear to keep it a secret?" He bobbed his head. "No, I mean you've got to swear an oath."

He raised his right paw. "I swear an oath, Hank. My lips are sealed."

"Okay, I guess I can trust you. You know what undercover work is?"

"Sort of."

"Well, that's what I was doing. See, we weren't getting anywhere with the chickenhouse murders, and I figgered the only way we could crack the case was for me to infiltrate the coyote tribe. It was risky. I knew there was a good chance I'd never come back alive, but it had to be done."

"No fooling?"

"That's right. And it had to be top secret. I mean, I couldn't even let you in on it. If them coyotes had ever suspected a thing, it would have been curtains for this old dog."

"Wow. Weren't you scared?"

"Naw. Well, a little bit. Actually, the toughest problem was keeping the women away."

"The women?"

"Right. Drover, you won't believe this, but they was actually fighting over me. I mean, it got embarrassing after a while. Why, one evening these two beautiful women . . . I'll tell you about it some other time. Right now we've got another case to crack. Now look at these tracks. What do you make of them?"

Drover squinted at the tracks. "Well, they were made by an animal, and I'd say the animal walked right past here and left these tracks in the dirt."

"So far, so good. Keep going."

He shook his head. "That's all I see, Hank. I'm stumped."

"Okay, now listen and learn. Them's badger tracks. While we was busy fighting off the whole coyote nation, a badger slipped into the ranch, and I've got an idea that he's still around."

"You mean . . . if we follow the tracks, we'll find him?"

"That's correct.

"Uh-oh. Badgers are pretty tough."

"Yes, that's true, but duty's duty. If we start letting badgers in here, before you know it they'll try to take the place over. Come on, Drover, we've got work to do."

He gulped. "Badgers have big claws, Hank."

"You leave the claws to me. I'll go in the first wave, then you jump him from behind. And dang you, if you run off and leave me again, I'll . . . I don't know what I'll do, but you won't like it."

"Okay, Hank. I'll be right behind you."

I put my nose to the ground and started following the trail. It led around the saddle shed and through the garden. Reading the signs, I saw where Mr. Badger had stopped in the garden and dug up a couple of worms or bugs.

I continued east, following the trail through the gate, past the gas tanks, up the hill, and right to the yard fence.

"This is worse than I thought, Drover. He's in the yard. That doesn't leave us much choice. This could get nasty, could be a fight to the death."

"Whose death?"

"In this business, you never know. You just have to give your best for the ranch. Come on, let's move out."

We hopped over the fence. I got down in my stalking position and picked up the trail again.

The scent was getting stronger now. It was *real* strong. Badgers have musk glands, you know, and they leave a heavy scent.

Suddenly I saw him, hiding in a bunch of

flowers. I froze. Drover ran into me. "This is it," I whispered. "Good luck."

I crept forward two more steps, went into my attack position, and sprang.

Suspended in the air over the flowerbed, I got a good look at the enemy. It suddenly occurred to me that badgers aren't black with two white stripes running down the middle of their backs. They don't have a small head with beady little eyes, or a long bushy tail.

It was a skunk. I had been duped.

I tried to change course in midair but it was too late. Out of the corner of my eye, I saw Drover jump the yard fence and head for the machine shed.

What followed was entirely predictable. I landed right in the middle of the scoundrel. He fired. The air turned yellow and poisonous. My eyes began to water and I gasped for breath.

Sally May's south window happened to be open. Was that my fault? I mean, had I gone through the house that morning opening all the windows? Of course not, but on this ranch, Rule Number One is that, when in doubt, blame Hank.

I ran for my life and rounded the corner of the house just as Sally May came boiling out the back door. She was armed with a broom and took a

swat at me as I flew past. My eyes were stinging so badly that I . . .

You've got to understand that I could hardly see and was having trouble catching my breath. The back porch door was open, and you might say that I ran into the utility room . . . where Sally May had just taken a basket of clean clothes out of the washing machine.

Was it *my* fault that she happened to be washing clothes that day?

"GET OUT OF MY HOUSE, YOU STINKING DOG!"

Well, as I've said before, every dog in this world isn't cut out for security work. It requires a keen mind, a thick skin, and a peculiar devotion to duty. I mean, you put in sixteen-eighteen hours a day. You're on call day and night. Your life is on the line every time you go out on patrol. You're doing jobs that nobody else wants to do because of the danger, etc.

You make the world a little safer, a little better. You take your satisfaction where you can get it, in knowing that you're doing the job right.

The very people you're protecting won't understand. They'll blame you when things go wrong. But that's the price of greatness, isn't it? And if you were born a cowdog, it's all part of a day's work.

Have you read all of Hank's adventures?

Join Hank the Cowdog's Security Force

Are you a big Hank the Cowdog fan? Then you'll want to join Hank's Security Force. Here is some of the neat stuff you will receive:

Welcome Package
- A Hank paperback embossed with Hank's top secret seal
- Free Hank bookmarks

Eight issues of *The Hank Times* with
- Stories about Hank and his friends
- Lots of great games and puzzles
- Special previews of future books
- Fun contests

More Security Force Benefits
- Special discounts on Hank books and audiotapes
- An original Hank poster (19" x 25") absolutely free

Total value of the Welcome Package and *The Hank Times* is $23.95. However, your two-year membership is **only $8.95** plus $3.00 for shipping and handling.

☐ Yes I want to join Hank's Security Force. Enclosed is $11.95 ($8.95 + $3.00 for shipping and handling) for my **two-year membership**. [Make check payable to Maverick Books.]

Which book would you like to receive in your Welcome Package? Choose from books 1–30.

(#   )   (#   )

FIRST CHOICE   SECOND CHOICE

                                                 BOY or GIRL

YOUR NAME   (CIRCLE ONE)

MAILING ADDRESS

CITY   STATE   ZIP

TELEPHONE   BIRTH DATE

E-MAIL

Are you a ☐ Teacher or ☐ Librarian?

Send check or money order for $11.95 to:

Hank's Security Force
Maverick Books
PO Box 549
Perryton, Texas 79070

DO NOT SEND CASH. NO CREDIT CARDS ACCEPTED.
Allow 4–6 weeks for delivery.

The Hank the Cowdog Security Force, the Welcome Package, and The Hank Times *are the sole responsibility of Maverick Books. They are not organized, sponsored, or endorsed by Penguin Putnam Inc., Puffin Books, Viking Children's Books, or their subsidiaries or affiliates.*

The Further Adventures
of Hank the Cowdog

The ranch is under attack!

"Now, what's that noise?"

Drover looked up in the trees and rolled his eyes. "I don't hear any..." And right then he heard the roar. His eyes got as big as saucers and he started to shiver. "What is it, Hank?"

"I don't know, but we're fixing to find out. I've got a hunch that it's a silver monster bird."

I turned my head for just a second, and when I looked back, Drover was gone. At first I thought he might have headed for the machine shed, but then I saw his gunnysack quivering. "Get out from under there! We've got work to do. I'm putting this ranch under Red Alert."

"But Hank, that thing roars!"

The roar was getting louder all the time. "Come on, son, it's time for battle stations. If that bird lands, it's liable to be a fight to the death."

The Further Adventures
of Hank the Cowdog

John R. Erickson

Illustrations by Gerald L. Holmes

Puffin Books

PUFFIN BOOKS
Published by the Penguin Group
Penguin Putnam Books for Young Readers,
345 Hudson Street, New York, New York 10014, U.S.A.
Penguin Books Ltd,
27 Wrights Lane, London W8 5TZ, England
Penguin Books Australia Ltd,
Ringwood, Victoria, Australia
Penguin Books Canada Ltd,
10 Alcorn Avenue, Toronto, Ontario, Canada M4V 3B2
Penguin Books (N.Z.) Ltd,
182-190 Wairau Road, Auckland 10, New Zealand

Penguin Books Ltd, Registered Offices:
Harmondsworth, Middlesex, England

First published in the United States of America
by Maverick Books, Gulf Publishing Company, 1983
Published by Puffin Books, a member of
Penguin Putnam Books for Young Readers, 1999

20 19 18 17 16 15 14 13 12 11

LIBRARY OF CONGRESS CATALOGING-IN-PUBLICATION DATA
Erickson, John R.
The further adventures of Hank the Cowdog / John R. Erickson ;
illustrations by Gerald L. Holmes.
p. cm.
Originally published in series: Hank the Cowdog ; 2.
Summary: Hank the Cowdog almost loses his job as Head
of Ranch Security when he develops a case of Eye-crosserosis.
ISBN 0-14-130378-6 (pbk.)
[1. Dogs—Fiction. 2. West (U.S.)—Fiction. 3. Humorous stories.
4. Mystery and detective stories.] I. Holmes, Gerald L., ill. II. Title.
III. Series: Erickson, John R. Hank the Cowdog ; 2.
PZ7.E72556Fu 1999 [fic]—dc21 [II 1b11 08-27-98] 98-41812 CIP AC

Printed in the United States of America

To my children,
Scot, Ashley, and Mark

CONTENTS

CHAPTER ONE

The Silver Peril

It's me again, Hank the Cowdog. As I recall, it was the 14th of May when the silver monster bird swooped down on the ranch and threatened us with death and destruction.

Or was it May 15th? Could have been the 16th. Anyway...

Silver monster birds are huge creatures with a body that's long and skinny, resembles the body of a snake, which makes me think they might be a cross-breed between a bird and a reptile. The head sort of confirms that, because it has a sharp nose and two wicked eyes.

In other words, it ain't your usual bird head. Oh yes, did I mention that they don't have a beak? No beak whatsoever. That's a pretty important clue right there. It ain't natural. Show me a bird without a beak and I've got some questions to ask him.

Another thing about the silver monster birds is that they have shiny feathers—not your usual dull brown or glossy black, but bright, shiny silver feathers. And a lot of the monster birds will have a white marking on the side which resembles a star.

They have big drooping wings with several things growing out of the underside. I call them "things" because I don't have a technical term for them yet. Whatever they are, starlings and blackbirds and sparrows don't have them. They may be poison stingers, I don't know.

These silver monster birds don't flap their wings. They glide like a buzzard or a hawk. And did I mention that they roar? Yes sir, they roar, and I mean LOUD. Your ordinary bird doesn't do that. He might cheep or squawk or sing a little tune, but you very rarely find one that roars.

It's the roar that makes the silver monster birds a little scary. It takes a special kind of dog to stand up to that roar, hold his ground, and keep on barking. I suspect that even some cowdogs would run from that terrible sound, but on this ranch we don't run *from* danger. We run *to* it.

Anyway, one day last week I caught a silver monster bird trying to slip onto the ranch. He should have known he couldn't get away with it. I mean, that roar is a dead give-away. My ears are very sensitive to certain sounds and there aren't too many roars that get past me.

Drover and I had put in a long night patrolling headquarters, fairly routine, as I recall. About the only excitement came a little after midnight when Drover got into a scuffle with a cricket. I told him to save his energy for bigger stuff. I mean, crickets cause a certain amount of damage around the place, but they ain't what you'd call a major threat.

I figger Pete can handle the cricket department and we'll take care of the more dangerous assignments. 'Course the problem with that is that Pete won't do it. Too lazy. He's a typical cat, but I don't want to get started on cats.

Anyway, Drover and I came in from night patrol and bedded down under the gas tanks. I scratched around on my gunnysack and got it fluffed up just right and had curled up for a long nap, when all at once I heard it.

My right ear went up. My ears are highly trained, don't you see, and they sort of have a mind of their own. I can be dead asleep and lost in beautiful dreams, but those ears never sleep.

They never go off duty. (This is fairly typical of your blue-ribbon, top-of-the-line cowdogs.)

I suppose I was dreaming about Beulah again. Derned woman is hard to get off my mind. I don't let women distract me during working hours, but sometimes I lose control when I'm asleep. I mean, a guy can keep an iron grip on himself only so long. Every once in a while he kind of goes to seed.

Well, I heard the roar. My right ear went up. My left ear went up. I glanced around. "Beulah?"

My sawed-off, short-haired, stub-tailed assistant lifted his head and stared at me. "I'm not Beulah. I'm Drover."

I studied the runt for a second, and my head began to clear. "I know who you are."

"How come you called me Beulah?"

"I didn't."

"I'm almost sure you did."

"Drover, *almost sure* might be close enough for some lines of work, but in the security business you have to be positive. You need to work on that."

"Okay, Hank."

"Now, what's that noise?"

Drover looked up in the trees and rolled his eyes. "I don't hear any..." And right then he heard the roar. His eyes got as big as saucers and he started to shiver. "What is it, Hank?"

4

"I don't know, but we're fixing to find out. I've got a hunch that it's a silver monster bird."

I turned my head just for a second, and when I looked back, Drover was gone. At first I thought he might have headed for the machine shed, but then I saw his gunnysack quivering.

"Get out from under there! We've got work to do. I'm putting this ranch under Red Alert."

"But Hank, that thing roars!"

The roar was getting louder all the time. "Come on, son, it's time for battle stations. If that bird lands, it's liable to be a fight to the death."

"But Hank, I . . . my foot hurts and I got a headache."

I took a corner of his gunnysack in my teeth and jerked it away. And there was Drover, my assistant Head of Ranch Security, quivering like a tub full of raw liver. "Get up and stay behind me. This ain't drill. This is Red Alert."

"Okay, Hank, I'll try but . . . Red Alert's pretty serious, isn't it . . . oh, my foot hurts!"

I took the lead and went streaking out into the pasture south of the house. I headed straight to the big dead cottonwood between the house and the creek and set up a forward position. I could see him now, coming in low over the hills and heading straight toward us.

It was a silver monster bird, all right, one of the biggest I'd ever seen. He had his big droopy wings out and his eyes were going back and forth across the ground. He was looking for something to swoop down on and kill. I could see that right off. I mean, if you've seen as many of these monster birds as I have, you sort of learn to read their thoughts.

This one had murder on his mind.

"Okay, Drover, listen up. I don't want to repeat myself. We've got steers in this home pasture. That's what the monster bird's after, them steers. He's gonna try to swoop down and pick up a steer and fly off with him."

Drover's teeth were chattering. "A whole steer!"

"Yes sir. They dive down and snatch 'em up and eat 'em in the air, and I mean bones and hair and teeth, ears, tail, everything. It's our job to keep him from doing that."

"What would he do . . . if he caught a dog instead of a steer?"

"We don't have an answer to that question."

"I . . . I'd kind of like to know before we do anything radical."

"Use your imagination."

"My leg hurts, Hank. I think I better . . ."

6

"Stand your ground and listen. When I count to three, we'll go over the top and let him have it. Don't save anything back. If he comes in low enough, we'll try to grab him.

"*Grab him!* But Hank, what would we do with him?"

I studied on that for a second. I hadn't thought that far ahead. "I guess just bite and scratch and fight for your life. You ready?"

"No."

"Well, ready or not, this is it—combat, Red Alert." I peeked over the top of the log. He was heading straight toward us.

"Oh my gosh, Hank, look how big he is, and his eyes, and his wings are smoking!"

"One!"

"Hank, my leg . . ."

"Two!"

". . . is killing me."

"Three! Attack, Drover! Charge! Bonzai!"

I leaped over the dead tree and threw myself into the monster bird's path. It was him or me. I bared my fangs and set up a ferocious bark, probably the ferociousest bark I ever made.

The roar was deafening. I mean, it shook the ground. Never heard anything quite so loud or frightful in all my career. No ordinary dog could

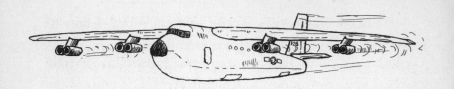

have stood his ground against that thing.

He kept coming, so I leaped into the air and snapped at him. Another foot or two and I might have put a fang-lock on him, but when he saw my teeth coming at him, he made the only sensible decision and quit the country.

I mean, he pointed himself north and evacuated, and he never looked back. The smoke and roar faded into the distance.

"And don't you ever try that again!" I yelled at

him as he went past. "Next time, you won't get off so easy."

I turned to Drover. He was lying flat on the ground with his paws over his ears. His eyes were shut tight. He wouldn't get no medals for bravery, but at least he hadn't run.

"Okay, Drover, you can come out now."

"Are we dead?"

"Nope. Against near impossible odds, we just whipped a silver monster bird."

Drover cracked his eyes, looked around in a full circle, and sat up. "How bad was it?"

"How bad? Almost beyond description, Drover. When he had me in his claws . . ."

"He had you in his claws, no fooling?"

"You didn't see it? Yup, he had these enormous claws with big hooks on the end, and he reached down and grabbed me."

"What did you do?"

"What did I do? Well, I called on an old trick that my granddaddy once told me about. I tore off his whole leg and left him with a bloody stump."

"You did?"

"Certainly did. Why do you think he flew away in such a hurry? I mean, that bird was scared when he left out of here, and I have my doubts that we'll ever see him again."

9

Drover looked around. "Where's the leg?"

"Oh, it's around here somewhere. We'll run into it one of these days. Can't miss it. Heck, it was almost as big as this tree."

"You want me to look for it?"

"Not now. I don't know about you, Drover, but I'm ready to shower out and shut her down for a few hours. I think we've earned ourselves some sleep."

And with that, we headed for our favorite spot on the ranch, the place just west of the house where the septic tank overflows and forms a beautiful pool of green water.

CHAPTER TWO

Egged On by Pete

In the security business, you learn to live your life a day at a time because you never know if you'll make it past that next monster. Any one of them is liable to be your last.

A lot of dogs can't handle that kind of pressure, but there's others of us who kind of thrive on danger. When you're in that category, you learn to savor the precious moments. I mean the little things that most dogs take for granted.

Like a roll in the sewer after a big battle. There's nothing quite like it, believe me. You come in hot and bloody and tore up and wore out, proud of yourself on the one hand but just derned near exhausted on the other hand, and you walk up to that pool of lovely green water and ... well, it's

11

hard to describe the wonderfulness of it.

That first plunge is probably the best, when you step in and plop down and feel the water moving over your body. Then you roll around and kick your legs in the air and let your nose feast on that deep manly aroma.

Your poodles and your Chihuahuas and your other varieties of house dogs never know the savage delight of a good ranch bath. If they ever found what they're missing, they'd never be the same again. There's just something about it that makes a dog proud to be a dog.

Well, I climbed out of the sewer and shook myself and sat down in the warm sunshine. Drover was still standing in water up to his knees. I noticed that he hadn't rolled around in it. He never does. He just wades in and stands there, looking stiff and uncomfortable.

"How do you expect to get clean if you don't get yourself wet?"

He wrinkled his nose. "I don't like to get wet."

"This water has special power, son. It revives the spirit."

He kind of dipped down and got his brisket wet and scampered out on dry land. "There. I feel much better now."

I just shook my head. Sometimes Drover acts

more like a cat than a cowdog. Makes me wonder . . . oh well.

We sunned ourselves for a few minutes, then
headed on down to the gas tanks. I had a gunnysack bed down there with my name on it and I
was all set to pour myself into it. I was fluffing it
up again and getting it arranged just right when
I heard the back door slam up at the house.

I perked my ears and listened. When the back
door slams at that hour of the morning, it often
means that Sally May has busted the yoke on
Loper's breakfast egg. He won't eat busted eggs,
for reasons which I don't understand. Seems to
me that an egg's an egg, and after a guy chews it
up and swallers it, it's all about the same anyway.

But Loper doesn't see it that way, which is fine
with me because around here, in Co-op dog food
country, an egg in any form is a gourmet delight.

I cut my eyes toward Drover. He had his chin
resting on his front paws and was drifting off to
sleep. He hadn't heard the door slam, and I didn't
see that it was my duty to tell him about it.

I slipped away from the gas tanks and loped
up the hill. Had my taste buds all tuned up for a
fried egg when I met Pete. He was going the same
direction I was.

"Get lost, cat. Nobody called your name."

He gave me a hateful look and hissed. Well, you know me. I try to live by the Golden Rule: "Do unto others but don't take trash off the cats." Pete was in the market for a whipping, seemed to me, so I obliged him. Figgered I might as well get it over with, while it was fresh on both our minds.

I jumped him, rolled him, buried him, cuffed him a couple of times, and generally gave him a stern warning about how cats are supposed to behave. After I'd settled that little matter, I trotted up to the yard gate, ready for my egg.

Sally May was standing there with her hands on her hips. I sat down and swept the ground with my tail, gave her a big smile and sat up on my back legs.

I picked up this little begging trick some years ago. It was pretty tough to learn—I mean, it takes balance and coordination and considerable athletic ability—but it's paid off more than once. People seem to love it. They like to see a dog beg for what they're going to give him anyway. Don't ask me why, but they do.

Begging sort of goes against my grain. I mean, my ma was no ordinary mutt. She had papers and everything and cowdog pride was sort of bred into me. But a guy has to make a living, and now and then he finds himself cutting a few corners.

Well, I went up on my hind legs. Sometimes I get my balance the first time and sometimes I don't. This time it worked. I balanced myself on two legs, and then to add a special touch, I wagged my tail and moved my front paws at the same time.

I don't believe the trick could have been done any better. It was a real smasher.

15

I was so busy with the trick that I didn't notice the sour look on Sally May's face. "Hank, you big bully! You ought to be ashamed of yourself for picking on that poor cat!"

"HUH?"

"Just for that, you don't get this egg. Here, Pete, kitty, kitty, kitty."

In a flash, Pete was there. I mean, when it comes to freeloading, he has amazing speed. He gave me a surly grin and went through the gate and started eating my egg. That really hurt.

Sally May gave Kitty-Kitty a nice motherly smile, then she turned a cold glare on me. "And besides being a bully, you smell *awful*."

How could she say that? I had just taken a bath, shampooed, the whole nine yards. I mean, a guy can't spend his whole life taking a bath. He's got to get out sometimes and when he does it's just natural that he picks up a few of the smells of the earth.

Besides that, I knew for a fact that Pete hadn't taken a bath in *years*. He hated water even more than Drover did. And he had dandruff too. You could see it all over him, looked like he'd been in a snowstorm.

What kind of justice do you have when a dog that takes a bath every day, and sometimes two or three times a day, gets accused of smelling bad, and a rinky-dink cat . . . oh well.

Pete was chewing my egg, and every now and then he'd turn his eyes toward me and give me a grin. Let me tell you, it took tremendous self-discipline for me to sit there and watch, when all of my savage instincts were urging me to tear down the fence and pulverize the cat.

Sally May went back into the house. I should have left right there, just walked away and tried to forget the whole thing. But I didn't.

Pete had laid down in front of the plate. I mean, he was too lazy to stand up and eat. He was purring and flicking the end of his tail back and forth and chewing every bite twenty-three times.

I found myself growling, just couldn't help it. His head came up. "Hmmm, you hungry, Hankie? You'd like this egg. It just melts in your mouth."

"No thanks, I got better things to do." That was the truth. I did. But I stayed there.

Pete shrugged and went on eating. I watched, and before I knew it, I was drooling at the mouth.

Pete got up, took a big stretch, and ambled over to where I was. He started rubbing against the fence. He was so close, I could have snatched him baldheaded, which I wanted to do very sincerely, only there was a wire fence between us.

"I'm not sure I can eat all that egg," he said. "I'm stuffed. You want the rest of it, Hankie?"

I should have said no. I mean, a guy has his pride and everything. But my mouth went to watering at the thought of that egg and . . . "Oh, I might . . . yeah, I'll take it."

He grinned and ambled back to the plate. He picked up the egg in his mouth and brought it over to the fence and dropped it right in front of my nose.

Well, I wasn't going to give him a chance to reconsider, so I made a grab for it. Hit the derned fence with the end of my nose.

But it was right there in front of me. I mean, I could smell it now, it was so close. It was giving off warm waves and delicious smells. I could even smell the butter it had been cooked in.

I made another snap at it, hit the fence and scabbed up my nose. Made my eyes water. When my vision cleared up, I saw Pete sitting there and grinning. I was losing patience fast.

"Gimme that egg. You said I could have it."

"Here, I'll move it a little closer." He got his nose under the egg and nudged it right against the fence.

Well, I just *knew* I could get it now, so I made

another lunge for it. Got a taste of it this time, but also wrecked my nose on that frazzling wire. I could see a piece of skin sticking up, right out toward the end.

"Gimme that egg!"

He licked his paw and purred.

Okay, that settled it. I'll fool around and nickel-and-dime a problem for a while, but there comes a time when you've got to get down to brute strength.

I backed off and took a run at it and hit the fence with all my speed and strength. I expected at least two posts to snap off at the ground, and it wouldn't have surprised me if I had taken out the whole west side.

Them posts turned out to be a little stouter than I thought, and you might say that the wire didn't break either. The collision shortened my backbone by about six inches and also came close to ruining my nose.

"Gimme that egg, cat, or I'll . . ."

Pete threw a hump into his back and hissed, right in my face. That was a serious mistake. No cat does that to Hank the Cowdog and lives to tell about it.

I started barking. I snarled, I snapped, I tore at the fence with my front paws, I clawed the ground. I mean, we had us a little riot going, fellers, and it was only a matter of time until Pete died a horrible death.

And through it all, I could still smell that egg, fried in butter.

The back door flew open and Loper stormed out. He had shaving cream on one side of his face and the other side was bright red.

"HANK, SHUT UP! YOU'RE GONNA WAKE UP THE BABY!"

I stopped barking and stared at him. Me? What had I . . . if it hadn't been for the cat . . .

I heard the baby squall inside the house. Sally May exploded out the door. "Will you tell your dog to shut up! He just woke the baby."

"Shut up, Hank!"

Shut up, Hank. Shut up, Hank. That's all anybody ever says to me. Not "good morning, Hank," or "thanks for saving the ranch from the silver monster bird, Hank, we really appreciate you risking your life while we were asleep." Nothing like that, no siree.

Well, I can take a hint. I gave Pete one last glare, just to let him know that his days on this earth were numbered, and I stalked back to the gas tanks.

I met Drover halfway down the hill. He'd just

pried himself out of bed. "What's going on, Hank? I heard some noise."

I glared at him. "You heard some noise? Well, glory be. It's kind of a shame you didn't come a little sooner when you might have made a hand."

"You need some help?"

I glanced back up the hill. Sally May was still out in the yard, talking to her Kitty-Kitty. "Yeah, I need some help. Go up there and bark at the cat."

"Just . . . just bark at the cat, that's all?"

"That's all. Give it your best shot."

"Any special reason?"

"General principles, Drover."

"Well, okay. I'll see what I can do."

He went skipping up the hill and I went down to the gas tanks to watch the show.

Maybe it was kind of mean, me sending Drover up there on a suicide mission, when he was too dumb to know better. But look at it this way: I get blamed for everything around here, and most of the time I don't deserve it. I figgered it wouldn't hurt Drover to get yelled at once or twice, and it might even do him some good.

Getting yelled at is no fun, but it does build character. Drover needed some character-building. That was one of his mainest problems, a weak character.

So I watched. The little runt padded up to the fence, plopped down, sat up on his back legs, and started yipping. Sally May put her hands on her hips, gave her head a shake, and said, "Well, if that isn't the cutest thing!"

She pitched him my egg and he caught it in the air and gulped it down.

A minute later, he was down at the gas tanks. "I did what you said, Hank, and I won a free egg. Are you proud of me?"

I was so proud of him, I thought about blacking both his eyes. But I was too disgusted. I just went to sleep.

That seems to be the only thing I can do around here without getting yelled at: sleep.

CHAPTER THREE

Stricken with Eye-Crosserosis

I slept until late morning, maybe ten o'clock or so. What woke me up was Drover's wheezing.

He wheezes in his sleep, don't you see, and makes a very peculiar sound. Sometimes I can sleep through it and sometimes I can't. As a general rule, I'm a light sleeper. That's one of the prices you pay for having sensitive ears. You hear every sound in the night, including some you'd rather not.

Don't know what causes Drover's problem. He claims he's allergic to certain weeds. Maybe so. He's also allergic to hard work and danger in any form. Anyhow, there's definitely something wrong with his nose.

And speaking of noses, mine was in poor

shape after that tussle with Pete and the wire fence. The black leathery part was all scraped up. By crossing my eyes like this . . . well, you can't see—by crossing my eyes I could sight down my nose and see the little flaps of skin rolled up.

I studied the damage for a long time. Kind of made me sad to see my old nose banged up that way. It's a well-known fact that a cowdog tends to be a little vain about his nose.

On the one hand it's a very delicate piece of equipment. On the other hand it's an object of beauty. Entire books have been written about the natural beauty of a cowdog's nose—or if they haven't been written, they ought to be. I bet they'd sell millions of copies and make somebody tubs full of money.

They used to tell that my Uncle Beanie packed his nose in mud every night. He lived to a ripe old age, and right up to the last the women were just nuts about him. He said it was his nose, said the mud treatment kept it soft and pretty.

Anyway, I sat there looking at my nose and listening to Drover wheeze and had my eyes crossed for a long time. And you know what?

They got hung up—my eyes, I mean. I couldn't get them uncrossed. It's a serious condition called Eye-Crosserosis.

Kind of throwed a scare into me. I shook my head and tossed it up and down. Didn't help, eyes stayed crossed. I hit the side of my head with my left paw and that didn't help, so I scratched at it with my hind leg. Nuthin. I was getting a little concerned by this time, because my eyes being crossed throwed everything out of focus, don't you see, which sort of left the ranch defenseless.

Ma used to tell us not to cross our eyes when we were pups, said they might not go back to normal. I never believed her, but she was right.

Well, I finally decided I'd better sound the alarm. "Drover, wake up, we're in a world of trouble." He wheezed and snored, didn't wake up. "Drover! Get up, son, this is no time to sleep. We could be on the brink of a disaster."

His head came up and he opened his eyes. "Beulah?"

"Beulah!"

He blinked a couple of times. "You're not Beulah."

"I'm certainly not, and what do you mean, dreaming about *my* woman? You got no right . . . look at me, Drover, and tell me what you see."

He studied me for a long time, squinted one eye and then the other, looked me up one side and down the other.

"Well, what do you see? Go ahead and say it, just spit it out."

"A dog."

"Look deeper. Details."

He looked deeper. "A cowdog?"

"The face, Drover, study the face."

He cocked his head. "Oh yeah, I see it now. It looks terrible, Hank."

"I was afraid of that. It's pretty obvious, huh?"

"Sure is."

"Do you think I look disfigured? I mean, I don't want to go around looking like a loon or a freak or something."

"I'd say you look kind of disfigured, Hank."

That was discouraging news. I tried walking around and ran into one of the legs on the gas tanks. "The worst part of it is that it's messed up my vision. Can't see worth a rip."

"Huh. That's really strange, Hank. I wouldn't have thought it would do that."

"Oh, it's not so strange, when you think about it. What do you reckon I ought to do to cure it?

"Beats me. Maybe a mud pack would help."

When a guy can't see, he'll try most anything. I followed Drover down to the sewer and he helped me up to the edge of the water. I dug balls of mud with my paws and plastered them over both eyes. Then I laid down to let the healing set in.

Must have laid there for half an hour. "What do you think now, Drover? Have we waited long enough?"

"Well . . . it still looks the same to me. Maybe you better go another hour."

"Maybe so." About fifteen minutes later, I began to think about what he'd said. "Wait a minute.

What do you mean, it still looks the same?" I heard him snore and wheeze. "Drover, wake up! What do you mean, it still looks the same to you?"

"Huh, what? What do I mean? Well, I guess that means it don't look any different."

"What are you talking about?"

"Your nose. It still looks beat-up and scabby to me."

"My nose! I wasn't talking about my nose, you little dunce."

"Oh."

"How could a scabby nose have anything to do with my vision?"

"I wondered about that."

I scraped off the mud and opened my eyes. I saw two Drovers staring at me. "It didn't help. I'm still afflicted."

"Hey! Your eyes are crossed!"

"Very good, Drover. It only took you . . . what, forty-five minutes to pick that up?"

"More like an hour."

"That's just great." I tried to think through my problem, one step at a time. "Well, this is a fine mess. What am I going to do now?"

"Well . . . if your eyes are crossed, maybe you could uncross 'em."

"What a wonderful idea, Drover."

"Yeah, it just came to me in a flash."

"I bet that was quite a flash."

"It was pretty good."

"Well, here's another flash. I already thought about that."

"You did?"

"And I tried it."

"You did?"

"And it didn't work."

"Oh."

"So do you have other flashes? I mean, with my eyes out of commission, this ranch is in real danger. If the coyotes ever got wind of this, we'd be almost helpless."

"Well . . . my eyes are pretty good. Maybe we could use my eyes and your judgment. How does that sound?"

I thought about that for a long time. I didn't want to rush into anything. Making cold, hard decisions is a very important part of being Head of Ranch Security. A guy just doesn't leap into those kinds of decisions.

"Maybe so. It may be our best shot. But remember: you're still working for me."

"Okay."

"You furnish the eyes and I'll furnish the brains, and . . ."

I stopped in the middle of the sentence. My left ear shot up. A pickup had just pulled in at the mailbox and was coming toward headquarters.

My reaction was completely automatic. I set up a bark and moved toward the sound and ran into Loper's roping dummy.

"Who is it, Drover, where are they, point me toward them, this could be serious stuff, *bark for Pete's sake,* sound the alarm!"

He let out his usual yip-yip-yip, which wouldn't have scared a fly, but I guess it was his best lick. "Okay, Hankie, follow me, here we go!"

Made me mighty uneasy, following Drover, but I didn't have much choice. We went tearing down the hill, me barking and Drover yipping. I kept right on his tail. I could see that much, even though it was double and out of focus.

All at once he came to a halt. I got myself shut down just in time, almost plowed him under. I mean, you get that much bulk and muscle going in high gear and you don't just stop on a dime.

Drover was spinning in circles and acting awfully strange. "Oh, Hank, I just can't go on, I never know what to say . . ."

"You're not supposed to *say* anything, son, just bark until we can check 'em out and give 'em clearance."

"But Hank, can you see who it is?"

I squinted and tried to focus on the pickup. About all I could come up with was that it was green. "No, who is it?"

"It's . . . Beulah."

My goodness, just the mention of her name made me weak and trembly in the legs, had to sit down and rest a minute.

"And Hank, there's somebody with her."

"It's . . ."

"Don't tell me, let me guess. Spotted bird dog, long skinny tail, kind of a goofy expression on his face?"

"Well . . . maybe so."

"It's Plato. She's been sweet on him for a long time and I've been waiting for a chance to clean house on him."

"What are we gonna do?"

"Stay behind me and stand by for further orders. We could get ourselves into a little skirmish here." I marched out into the lead and headed toward the pickup.

"Hank?"

"Later, son, I got violence on my mind."

"But Hank . . ."

I was too deep in concentration to be bothered with his yap. I marched up to the pickup and displayed my hardware. (In the security business, that's our way of saying that I showed him my teeth—teeth being the hardware, don't you see.)

I displayed my hardware. "So, fate brings us together at last, Plato. I thought you had better sense . . ."

"Hank."

"I thought you had better sense than to walk into my territory, Plato, but it's pretty obvious that I overestimated your intelligence."

"Hank?"

"Shut up, Drover. But seeing as how you were foolish enough to come on my ranch, I'm calling you out. Come on, let's have a little violence and bloodshed."

Well, that must have throwed a terrible scare into him. I mean, he didn't move a muscle or make a sound, not even a squeak. "What's the matter, Plato, you lose your voice all of a sudden? It's kind of embarrassing to get exposed in front of your girlfriend, ain't it?"

"Hank?"

I turned to the little noise-maker. "What?"

"You got the wrong pickup, Hank."

"HUH?"

"They're down at the corral."

I moved closer, sniffed the tires, checked out

the signs, gave it a thorough going over. "This is the wrong pickup, Drover, and since you're in charge of eyes now, I'll have to hold you responsible. I'm afraid this will go on your record. "

"But Hank . . ."

"Drover, there's only two kinds of pickups in this world: right ones and wrong ones. This is a wrong one. Study it carefully and memorize the signs. Next time, I'll expect better information."

"But Hank . . ."

"You think you can find the right pickup now?"

"I guess so."

"All right, let's move out. You can go first, take the scout position, but don't forget who's running the show."

"Okay, Hank, just follow me."

And with that, we marched down to the corral to attend the funeral of a certain spotted bird dog.

CHAPTER FOUR

Surprised, or You Might Even Say Shocked

We went ripping down to the corral, Drover in the lead and me coming along behind. I wasn't used to taking second place, and when we got close enough so's I could kind of make out the shape of the pickup, I moved up to my proper place.

"What about Plato? Is he trembling yet?"

Drover slowed to a walk. "No, he's not, Hank. As a matter of fact . . . are you sure Plato's a bird dog?"

"Sure I'm sure."

"He's got pointed ears."

"When I get done with him, he's liable not to have any ears."

"And big teeth."

"Big, but not big enough, Drover. It's common knowledge that bird dog teeth are dull."

"They sure look sharp."

"Looks are deceiving, son. In this business you learn to trust your instincts."

I reached the pickup, and right away I caught Beulah's scent. A train-load of flowers couldn't have smelled sweeter. There was just something about that woman . . . it's hard to explain.

You'd think a guy like me—hardboiled, tested in combat, just a whisker away from being a dangerous weapon—you'd think a guy like me wouldn't respond to the softer things in this life. But the scent of Beulah did peculiar things to me.

"Morning, ma'am, and welcome to the ranch. It's always a pleasure . . ." I stopped and stared at her. It appeared to me that she'd put on a lot of weight, and her coat looked rough as a cob. "What's come over you, Beulah? You've changed, you don't have a healthy look about you."

I mean, her hair looked terrible, as coarse as straw . . .

It *was* straw. I was talking to a bale of hay on the back end of the pickup bed, must have followed the wrong scent, I mean alfalfa hay smells a lot like . . . never mind.

I kind of meandered toward the front. That eye problem was causing me entirely too much grief, and it was pretty clear that I couldn't depend on Drover to steer me in the right direction.

Technically speaking, Drover was second in command on the place. Another way of putting it is that he was *last* in command.

Drover was hopping up and down and spinning in circles. "Hi, Beulah, gosh it's good to have you here on the ranch!"

"Well, thank you, Drover. It's good to see you boys again."

I put a shoulder into Drover and nudged him away. "'Scuse me, son, I'll handle the women if you don't mind." I looked up into her face and my old heart began to pound. Mercy! Those big brown eyes, that silky hair, those nice ears, that fine pointed nose. "Beulah, before you got here, the day was only beautiful. Now that you're here, it's almost unbearable."

"Well, isn't that nice." She smiled. "Thank you, Hank."

"On behalf of the security division, it's my pleasure to welcome you to the ranch. If there's anything we can do to make your stay more comfortable, more interesting, more exciting, or more of anything else your heart desires . . ."

"Hank, what on earth happened to your nose?"

"Oh, just a few routine battle scars, ma'am. We had a little tussle with a silver monster bird this morning, nothing to get alarmed about. Now, if you'd like to take a little walk down to the creek . . ."

"And your eyes . . . are they crossed?"

Drover hopped back into the conversation. "They sure are, but look at mine, Beulah!"

I gave him an elbow. "It's a temporary affliction, Beulah. Now . . ." I heard a growl, didn't sound like Beulah. "Was that you?"

"No, Hank, it was my . . . my companion."

"Was, huh? Well, speaking of your companion, I mean since you brought the subject up, let me say this. Number one, he ain't exactly welcome on this ranch. Number two, if he can lie still and keep his yap shut, I'll try to ignore him. But, number three, if he tries that growl business again, I'm liable to feed it to him for lunch."

Would you believe that he growled again? How dumb can a bird dog be? Well, I couldn't let it slide, even though I had better things to do than to clean Plato's plow.

"And number four, you might tell your friend to step over here and we'll get his whipping out of the way."

All at once Drover was there beside me. "Hank, be careful. I don't think you . . ."

"I'll handle it, son. You stand by to clean up the bird dog blood."

Plato pushed Beulah aside and leaned over the edge of the pickup. That kind of surprised me. I didn't think he'd take it that far. Anyway, he leaned out and growled again.

Turned out that Drover was right. Plato *did* have sharp teeth and he did have pointed ears. He'd changed since I'd seen him last.

Drover was hopping up and down, and he whispered in my ear. "Hank, I don't think that's Plato."

"Huh?"

"Is Plato a . . . Doberman pinscher?"

"*A Doberman pinscher!*" I glanced up at Plato. It was all clear now. I'd made an error. I looked over at Beulah. She seemed a little uneasy. "Who is this imposter?"

"His name is Rufus, and he just moved to our ranch, and be careful, Hank, because he's very mean."

"What happened to Plato?"

"He's back at the ranch. He's afraid to come out of the post pile because Rufus . . ."

Rufus took over from there, had kind of a nasty

deep voice. "Because I whip him on sight. It's my ranch now, and I don't like bird dogs. And I don't like cowdogs with scabby noses and crossed eyes. You got anything to say about that?"

I gave it some thought. Those teeth were awful big and awful sharp. "I figger there's room in this world for differences of opinion. It just happens that I don't care a whole lot for Doberman pinschers, so I guess we're about even."

"I always heard that cowdogs had a yellow streak."

I bristled at that, and it must have worried Beulah. "Hank, don't pay any attention to him. He's just a bully. Don't let him get you into a fight. That's what he wants."

She had a point there. "All right, Beulah, for

you I'll let it go. Come on, Drover, we've got work to do."

Drover took off like a little rocket, heading for the feed barn. I walked away at a dignified pace. I'd gone maybe twenty steps when I heard Rufus snarl.

"You got a big mouth, Beulah. When I want your opinion, I'll ask for it."

"My opinion is that you're a brute, and I wish you'd never come to the ranch."

"Well, you better get used to it, honey, because I'm the main man in your life now. Here, gimme a little kiss, just to let me know that you really care."

I stopped.

"Keep your paws off me, you you you animal!"

"Come on, honey, just a little one." Bam! She slapped him. "You shouldn't have done that, Beulah, you just shouldn't have done that."

I turned around. Rufus bristled up and started toward her, showing all of his teeth. "Come here, woman."

"Don't you touch me!"

I headed for the pickup. "I just changed my mind, Rufus. I don't think I like your attitude, so why don't you climb down here and I'll give you a kiss you won't forget."

He stopped and stared at me. And then he laughed. "You don't know what you're asking for, cowdog."

"Just a fair chance to take you apart."

He jumped to the ground and faced me.

"When you go against a Doberman, there ain't no fair chance. Just bad, worse, and disastrous."

"That's the kind of odds I like, Rufus. Come on."

"Hank, don't do it!" Beulah called. "Run away, don't try to be a hero."

I took a deep breath and looked at my lady. "It ain't a matter of trying, Beulah. To some of us it just comes natural."

I faced the enemy. I was seeing double, which wasn't so good since it was hard to judge which one to fight. I picked the one on the left, sucked in my gut, and made a dive for him.

It was the wrong one. I took a ferocious bite out of the blue sky, and while I was in the air, Rufus got me, and I can't finish the story.

I'm sorry, I hate to leave things hanging but I just can't tell the rest of it. Maybe Drover will write his memoirs one of these days and you can find out what happened.

So go on to chapter 5 but don't expect to find out about the fight.

CHAPTER FIVE

Top Secret Material

I changed my mind. Might as well go on and tell the awful truth.

I got whupped. There it is, right out in the open, and that's about the awfulest truth I can imagine.

In this big land of ours, there's a certain number of dogs that get whupped every day. But for cowdogs and heads of ranch security, it ain't a common occurrence. In fact, to some of us getting whupped is not only unpleasant, it's unthinkable.

I mean, you spend your life learning the security business. You learn tactics and strategy. You learn to use your eyes and nose and ears. You learn to cut for sign. You learn the difference between good and evil and you devote your life to protecting the good.

But fellers, it's hard to protect the good and combat evil when any old jake-legged mutt can come onto the ranch and give you a whupping. It sort of undermines your credibility.

Maybe I shouldn't pass along any classified information about the fight. I mean, I'm telling this story and I can tell it any way I choose, and I just might not choose to advertise the gloomy facts. What's to stop me from changing things around and saying that I whupped Rufus and ran him off the place, with his tail between his legs?

Well, in the first place it's fairly common knowledge that Doberman pinschers don't have tails because they've been chopped off. Don't ask me why, that ain't my department, all I can say is that some dogs get their tails chopped off, and when that happens it's not possible for them to get run off a ranch with their tail between their legs because they don't have a tail, don't you see.

In the second place, if I changed the story around it would be a big nasty LIE, and furthermore I get the feeling that I'm just rambling on to avoid telling about the fight which is still a very raw spot in my memory.

All right, it's time to get serious. I'd advise you to sit down, take a deep breath, and get a good hold on your chair, because what follows is liable to be the most electrifying, terrifying, scarifying, mortifying, disturbifying and shockifying stuff you ever read.

One last word of warning before we go on. I'd suggest you lock the doors and winders and draw the blinds, and don't let the kids read this. I don't want the children to know that I got whupped.

After you've read this chapter, please cut it out of the book and burn it. It's easy to do with a pair of scissors or a knife, just . . . oh well, I guess you can figger that part out.

All right, enough said, here we go. Get hold of something stout and hang on.

WARNING!!!

The following information is highly classified and may prove dangerous to certain individuals with high blood pressure, low blood sugar, or poor bladder control. It should be taken in small amounts and followed with periods of sleep. If unusual symptoms occur, please consult a physician immediately. You needn't consult a lawyer because dogs can't be sued.

Me and Rufus were squared off—by the way, are you sure the kids are gone and the doors are locked? Check again, just to be sure—me and Rufus squared off and faced each other.

You've seen Doberman pinschers up close and you know how ugly they are—sharp, pointed ears and big teeth and them nasty little eyes, remind you of something out of a nightmare. Well, that's what I was looking at.

Some people claim that a cowdog never knows fear. I've got to dispute that. There for a second, I felt a little stab of fear, yes I did, because I wasn't facing just one Doberman pinscher, I was facing two. Double vision.

Up in the pickup, Beulah was saying, "No, Hank, don't do it, run for your life, he'll tear you apart, he'll kill you!"

Rufus glared at me and grinned. "You ready for this, cowdog?"

I swallered. "Ready as I'll ever be."

"You sure you want to get mauled in front of Beulah? We could go down in the bushes and do it in private."

"Suit yourself, Rufus."

He shrugged. "Well, you had your chance." He turned to Beulah. "Pay attention, woman, this is what happens to dogs that cross Rufus."

Back to me. "Well, shall we dance?"

I sprang into action, made a dive for the image on the left, and as you already know, it was the wrong one. I got nothing but air, otherwise I might have . . . oh well.

Rufus caught me on the fly, when I was in midair, and put a deadly clamp on my neck. I tried to whirl around and get one of his ears but it was already too late. Once you get in the grip of a Doberman pinscher, you don't break out real easy.

That's where the name of the breed comes from, don't you see. They definitely pinch when they bite, so there you are, a little background material.

Well, once he had me in that deadly grip he pressed his advantage, which is just the sort of cheap trick you can expect from a dog that's bred and raised to be a professional bully. He throwed me to the ground. I leaped high in the air and we went around and around. But I still couldn't get out of his jaws.

Up in the pickup, Beulah was almost hysterical. "Rufus, stop it, oh please stop before someone gets hurt! Drover, do something!"

Drover had found himself a nice quiet spot inside the feed barn, but when she called he poked his head out and yipped a few times. I think you could say that Rufus wasn't worried.

Well, we snarled and growled and snapped and tore up a large area of ground, but I still couldn't get out of the pinchers. Then Rufus put me on the ground again. I was completely wore out from the struggle. I didn't have anything left. Also, I was beginning to think the unthinkable, that I'd been whupped on my own ranch, in front of my assistant and the lady of my dreams.

Rufus had them little eyes right down in my face. Ever notice a Doberman's eyes? They got no pity in them, no feeling, and up close they can give you the chills.

"Say calf-rope."

"Rain on you."

"Say that Beulah's an ugly hag."

"Never."

"Say that you're yella."

"No."

Beulah jumped out of the pickup. "Leave him alone, you horrible villain! Let him go!"

He turned his head and showed her some fangs. That gave me just enough time to wiggle out and get to my feet. We faced each other again.

"Hank, run for your life!" Beulah cried. "Don't be proud, run!"

"Cowdogs don't run, Beulah. We fight to the death."

Rufus took a step toward me. "That's the spirit. I hate to kill a dog against his will."

He crept toward me, all bunched up in his shoulders and his teeth gleaming in the sun. He had a grin on his face, which was sort of disconcerting, if you know what I mean. Made a guy think he enjoyed this stuff.

Well, I was still seeing double. Last time, I'd made a dive for the image on the left, so this time I went for the one on the right and it was wrong too. Don't know how to explain that. I mean, when you try both sides and still draw a black bean, what more can you do?

I dove at him and missed. He made a slash at my throat but got me by the scruff of the neck instead. I twisted around and managed to get one of his ears. I didn't tear it off but I put a wrinkle in it.

Drover came tearing out of the feed barn, slipped between two boards in the fence, and started running in circles around us, yipping as loud as he could.

"Get him, Drover!" I yelled. "This is the fight you've been saving up for, son!"

He made a dive at Rufus and nipped him on

the rump. Rufus whirled around and showed him a mouthful of teeth, which just about caused the little mutt to turn inside-out. He screeched and headed for the feed barn.

I piled into Rufus and thought I was getting the upper hand when he put a judo move on me, throwed me to the ground and landed on top of me.

I knew I was finished. I could hear Beulah crying.

Rufus got me by the throat, closed his jaws, and started digging in.

Well, as you might have guessed by now, he didn't kill me. All at once, Slim and High Loper and Billy (he lived on a ranch down the creek and always kept a bunch of mutts around, such as Plato and Rufus, and Beulah was the only good dog he'd ever owned, if you ask me), all at once, Slim and High Loper and Billy were there, yelling and trying to pull us apart.

"Here, Roof, down boy, hyah, cut that out!"

Billy took his pet dragon by the collar and dragged him a short distance away. Loper held me back. "Billy, that's quite a dog you've got there."

"He's bad, ain't he? I figgered I needed a dog around that could take care of business. Say, I thought old Hank was a better fighter than that."

Loper looked down at me. "So did I."

I wagged my tail and whimpered. Couldn't he see that my dadgum eyes were crossed? I mean, how can a dog fight with Eye-Crosserosis?

Loper didn't notice. "I guess he's showing his age. You don't think about these dogs getting old, but they do, same as the rest of us. Well, Hank, anything broke?"

Only my heart, but I didn't expect him to care about that.

"Well," Billy said, "guess I'd better take this beast home before he does any more damage. Y'all come see us."

"Sure will. Y'all too."

They got into the pickup and drove off. I'll never forget the expression on Beulah's face as they pulled out. She just looked at me with big sad eyes while Roof-Roof sat on the bale of hay like a king on his throne.

When they were gone, Loper reached down and rubbed me behind the ears. "Well, Hank, I guess you're not the top dog in the neighborhood anymore. Kinda hurts, don't it?"

Loper and Slim went back to work and left me there alone. It kinda hurt, yes it did.

(FINAL NOTE: Don't forget to destroy this chapter. And don't let the kids find out what happened.)

CHAPTER SIX

Drover Turns on the Dearest Friend He Has in This World

Everyone left and I limped and dragged myself toward the gas tanks, figgered I needed a long spell of rest because I was so sore and beat up from the fight.

I'd gone maybe twenty-five steps when it occurred to me that I couldn't see the gas tanks, didn't know exactly which way to go, and was too wore out to get there anyway.

I mean, that Doberman had given me a terrible beating. My throat hurt, my neck hurt, my ears had been chewed up. I was limping on one front leg and packing one of the back ones. When you were built to be a four-legged creature, it's hard to motivate on two.

I found the corral fence and followed it around to the gate in front of the saddle shed. That was as far as I could go. I flopped down and waited for help to arrive. I knew Drover would be along directly and he could lead me down to the gas tanks and help me into bed.

I waited and waited. Drover didn't show up. Couldn't understand that. You'd think the little guy would come around just as soon as he was sure the coast was clear. I mean, when the Head of Ranch Security is out of commission, that's cause for concern, right?

About half an hour later, I heard something off to the south. With considerable effort, I lifted my head and looked in that direction. Couldn't see anything but a blur, but my ears are pretty keen and I got a good reading on the sound.

It was kind of a click-click-click, made by a four-legged animal with a short stride. The click part came from little claws hitting the hard ground.

It was Drover, I knew it was. "Drover, I'm over here!"

I cocked my head and listened. Whoever it was didn't answer. He broke into a run and took off to the east, and in a minute the sound was gone.

That was strange. Why would Drover take off like that? Surely he knew I'd been beat up and needed some help.

Well, I thought about it and came up with an answer. Drover was out looking for me and with his poor vision and dead nose, he just hadn't located me yet. He'd find me after a bit.

But why had he run when he heard me call? That was a little harder to fit into the picture, but you know, when a guy wants the picture to come out right, he'll find ways of making it. Facts don't squeal when you stuff 'em where you want 'em to go.

I told myself that Drover was still shook up over the big fight and hadn't got his nerves under control yet. My voice had scared him. He'd come around after a while.

Well, the hours dragged on and still no Drover. The afternoon sun got blistering hot and the wind blew sand in my eyes. Along toward the end of the day, I was feeling mighty weak and thirsty and decided I'd better give up waiting for Drover. I mean, it might take him another half-day to find me.

So I pushed myself up on all two legs (I was packing the other two, remember) and limped over in front of the saddle shed door, where the cowboys were sure to find me when they shut down for the night. It couldn't have been more than ten-twelve steps, but it took all my energy just to get there.

I flopped down, curled up in a ball, and waited. Sure 'nuff, at sundown Slim and Loper came along and put their saddle-horses up for the night.

I was in perfect position. They couldn't put their saddles up without seeing me there, and I felt sure that once they saw my wretched condition, they'd give me some well-deserved sympathy and maybe carry me down to the gas tanks.

Slim pulled off his saddle and came up to the door. His eyes were red from the dirt and the wind, and he looked tired. "Move, Hank, I got to get in." I lifted my head and whapped my tail and whined, figgered that would give him a hint that I was stove up. "Well, suit yourself."

He opened the door, stepped over me, and went inside, dragging his saddle. I took a lick from all four cinches and both stirrups, and I mean that last one hurt.

Then Loper came. He looked down at me and muttered something under his breath, then he tried to walk over me and stepped on my tail and so naturally I yelped.

What's so bad about that? I mean, my tail's
alive and when you step on it it hurts, and when
it hurts I yelp. Seems reasonable to me.

But Loper stumbled and I guess he got sore
about it. "Hank, for crying out loud, do you have
to park yourself right in the middle of traffic?"

Slim came over to the door and looked down at
me. "He acts like he don't feel real good."

Well, at last we were getting somewhere. I whapped my tail to let 'em know that they were on the right track.

Then Loper said, "If he can't whip these dogs anymore, he's gonna have to learn to stay out of fights." They stepped over me and closed up the shed. "If you can't handle Billy's dog, then next time he comes around you better go to the house, you hear? When your body fails, you have to use your brain, if you've got one."

That's the kind of sympathy you get around this ranch. All they expect is a twenty-four hour day, a perfect record, and a pint of blood every now and then just to prove . . . oh well.

A guy can't afford to get worked up about injustice. It's worse than running rabbits.

Darkness fell and there I was, all alone, curled up in a ball of hair with the wind blowing dirt in my face. The moon came up and the coyotes started howling. If they'd known my condition, they could have ravaged the place, I mean swept down and pillaged it from one end to the other.

I could only hope they wouldn't launch an attack, because ranch security was at its most dangerous level in many years.

At last I drifted off to sleep. Don't recall what time it was when I woke up. I heard some noise out there between the saddle shed and the house. My usual response would have been to leap into action and sound the alarm, but I wasn't up to my usual response. I growled. That was about the best I could do.

"Who's out there? State your name and your business or I'll . . . who's there?"

There was a moment of silence, then I heard Drover's voice. "Hank? You okay?"

"No, I'm not okay, and what do you mean, creeping around in the night?"

"Oh! I was up and thought I ought to come check on you."

"Well you sure took your time getting here. Where the devil have you been?"

"I got busy with some things, Hank, and just never got around."

"Get over here, so I won't have to yell. My throat hurts."

He came closer but stopped about ten feet away. He seemed kind of uneasy about something. "This better?"

"Is there some reason why you can't come over here where I am? I ain't got scabies."

"I know that, but I . . . Hank, I don't want to see you this way. I guess that's why I didn't come around sooner."

"What do you mean by that? I'm the same Hank only a little beat up."

"That's what I mean. Beat up." He looked down at his feet and kind of shuffled around. "I've seen you fight monsters and coyotes and coons, and you always won. I guess I thought . . . you see what I mean?"

"Yeah, it's coming clear. A guy loses one fight and all his so-called friends think he's over the hill. Is that what you're saying?"

"It makes a guy wonder. I don't know what to think."

"Why you little pipsqueak! Just for that, I'm gonna . . ." I pushed myself up and started after him. Went two steps and fell down, just didn't have the energy to thrash him.

"That's what I mean, Hank. You ought to give me a licking for saying all this stuff . . . but you can't. I can do anything I want to do . . . but I don't know what I want to do. I'm all confused."

"You're definitely confused."

"But see, I know that if I wanted to stick my tongue out at you—like this—I could do it."

He did it, stuck his tongue out at me. "Watch it, Drover, you're breeding a scab on the end of your nose."

"And I got a suspicion that if I wanted to parade in front of you—like this—I could do it too."

And that's just what the runt did, paraded in front of me *and* stuck out his tongue. I took a snap at him, but he was out of my range.

"Drover, you're courting disaster."

"And Hank, I have an idea that I could even throw some dirt on you and get by with it."

"I wouldn't try that, son."

"I know you wouldn't, and I wouldn't either . . . only I just want to. Like this." He scratched the ground with his paw and threw dirt on me.

I couldn't believe he did that. On a better day, I would have torn him apart, I mean ripped him up one side and down the other. But I had to lie there and take it. I managed to growl, but that was my best lick.

"Okay, Drover, you did it. You happy now?"

"No, I feel awful, I hate myself, I just don't know what to think any more...only I bet I could do it again." And he did it again, threw dirt on me, stuck out his tongue, and went prancing back and forth.

Then he started crying. "Oh Hank, why did you have to get whipped? I was happy the way things were, but now I just feel like a louse! Tell me what to do."

I shook the dirt off. "All right, I'll tell you what to do. First thing, say you're sorry. Second thing, go up to the gas tank and say 'I will be more respectful to the Head of Ranch Security' a thousand times. And then go out on patrol and take care of the ranch."

"All of that?"

"Yes sir, every bit of it."

He rolled his eyes and looked up at the stars. "But Hank, I don't want to...and I don't have to...because you can't make me."

I stared at him. "Then why did you ask?"

"I don't know. I better go, Hank, before I make you mad."

"You're a little late for that, son."

He started backing away. "I'm sorry, Hank, I really am. I just wanted to find out . . ."

He took off and that was the last I saw of the sawed-off, stub-tailed, ungrateful little wretch. But all through the night I heard him. You think he was out on patrol? Taking care of the ranch? Keeping an eye on the chickenhouse? Checking for coons?

No sir, he was out there playing peekaboo with Pete the Barncat.

Tricked, Led Astray, and Abandoned to a Terrible Fate

I had thought that maybe I would be better come morning, but I was worse. Not only did I ache and throb from nose to tail, but I was getting weak from hunger and thirst.

And as if that wasn't enough, along about ten o'clock in the morning the ants and flies started moving in on me.

It started with a couple of big green flies buzzing around my ears. Well, you know me. I don't allow that, never have. I sat up and took defensive action. I snapped and growled and sent

one of them to fly heaven, which was very satisfying but not so good in the taste department.
Never did care for the taste of green flies.

The other one kept it up. Then there were two
and four and ten and twenty, and I was wore out
and couldn't keep them away. Finally I laid my
head down and gave up.

They crawled over my nose, buzzed in my
ears, walked around my eyes, and bit me on the
rump, which really hacked me off but I didn't
have the energy to fight back.

Then came the ants, those little black villains
that march in single file and contribute absolutely
nothing to this world, except they sting innocent
victims and drive you nuts. Why were they put on
this earth? You got me.

They came in rows and columns, marching up
to me in unending lines. I don't know what they
expected to find or why they singled me out, but
by ten-thirty I had become a major population
center for ants.

They crawled up my tail and just by George
moved in. They were in my hair, on my face,
inside my ears and nose and mouth, and when
they found something they didn't approve of, they
just stung it.

Hateful little things.

I tried to fight them off for a while, but there was no end to them, they just kept coming. I was too tired and weak and hungry to fight anymore, so I gave up. Heck, if they wanted to eat me alive, that was okay with me, long as I didn't have to put out any effort.

I guess it was around noon when Slim and Loper came around. I must have looked pretty ragged by then because I got their attention.

Loper bent down and started picking ants off my face. "Say, this dog's not doing any good. What's wrong, Hank?"

I lifted my head and gave him a wooden stare. What was wrong? I'd been defeated in battle, wounded, abandoned, mocked, and abused. I was thirsty, half-starved, windblown, sunburned, and tormented by ants and flies. My spirit was smashed, my heart was broken, and I didn't give a rip whether I lived or died.

Other than that, it was a pretty nice day.

Slim bent down too. I heard his knees pop. "Maybe we better get him some food, reckon? You want some grub, Hankie?"

Slim stayed at the saddle shed and Loper went up to the house. He came back with a bowl of milk and eggs. I would have preferred scrambled eggs. It takes too much energy to eat them raw. I mean, you got to chase down the slimy part and get a handle on it before you can eat it.

But in this life you don't always get your eggs scrambled.

I got to admit that the boys were pretty nice to me this time. I mean, it came about twenty-four hours too late, but at least they made an effort. They set the bowl down in front of my nose and went on to lunch.

I took a few bites and decided maybe it was worth the trouble of eating, when all at once guess who came along, rubbing up against the fence, purring like a little chain saw, and holding his tail high in the air. You got it. Pete.

I stopped eating and gave him a withering glare.

"Umm, hi, Hankie, time to eat?"

"Scram, cat. I got no time for your foolishness."

"Where'd you get all the flies?"

"I got lonesome."

He grinned and sharpened his claws on a fencepost. "What would you take for some milk and eggs, Hankie? I just *love* milk and eggs."

"I'd take one of your legs and about six inches off that tail. Beat it."

He looked at his claws and rubbed against the post and moved toward the bowl in his typical dumb-cat manner, purring and switching the tip of his tail.

I don't know what it is about that tail-switching, but it just don't sit right with me. There's something about it that gets me stirred up. I glared at him and growled.

He walked up to the edge of the bowl, flicked his paw into the milk, and licked it. "Ummm! That's mighty tasty, Hankie. How come they're giving you milk and eggs today? That's pretty plush treatment for a dog . . ." He turned and curled the end of his tail around my nose. ". . . that got whipped."

I snapped at him, missed amputating his tail by just a matter of inches. "I'll plush *your* treatment if you don't get that tail out of my face."

He grinned. "How come your eyes are crossed, Hankie?"

"It's the latest style."

"It must be hard to be cocky when you're cross-eyed, hmm?"

"I'll manage. Stick that tail over here one more time and I'll show you."

He did, I snapped, I missed, he grinned. "Strike two, Hankie. Your aim's not what it used to be. That's sure too bad because," he took a big stretch and dug his claws into the dirt, "because I just might try to steal your milk."

"You touch my milk and you're a dead cat."

"Bet you can't stop me."

I pushed myself up to a sitting position—with considerable effort, I might add—and prepared for combat. "You just try it."

He reached out his paw and touched the surface of the milk, ever so lightly. "I touched it."

He touched off a by-George explosion, is what he touched. I didn't think I had enough energy to romp a cat, but come to find out I did. I made a slash at him and missed. He walked away, flicking his tail and grinning at me over his shoulder.

"Strike three, Hankie. Bet you can't catch me."

I lunged at him and got him. Well, I got some hairs off the end of his tail, actually, but that was enough to make me want some more. I made another pounce at him.

He squirmed out of my grip and went padding across the pasture toward the creek. Ordinarily he would have made a dash for the nearest tree but this time he didn't.

Well, this gave me a valuable piece of information and I began to formulate an overall strategy and plan of battle, which is one of the normal procedures we use in the security business.

One of the major advantages a cowdog has over a cat is that your ordinary run-of-the-mill cat is flighty and impulsive, while your cowdog applies mental discipline to every problem. I think most experts would back me up on this.

I mean, let's face it: it's a well-known fact that cats act on whim and impulse and lack the mental whatever-it-is to think in terms of a long-range strategy. Some authorities would say they're fairly stupid animals, which is what I would say.

Pete's behavior offered a classic example of this. Instead of staying close to the big trees around the corral, he headed down toward the creek, where the trees tended to be small and scrubby: creek willows and tamaracks instead of elms and cottonwoods.

In other words, Pete had made a crucial mistake which any dog trained in security work would never make: he had become cocky and careless and had allowed himself to be lured away from his best defensive position.

Once I had my basic strategy in mind, I followed the cat out into the pasture and down into the creek willows, keeping him in sight and waiting for my big opportunity. We call this "lulling the enemy." As Uncle Beanie used to say, "Lull 'em to sleep and then wake 'em up in the rudest possible manner."

I must have stalked him for a mile or more, far enough from the house so that it was unfamiliar territory. I figured that was far enough. The time had come. The bell was tolling for whom the bell was tolling for.

He was maybe five feet in front of me. I gathered all my strength, threw it into one mighty lunge, and didn't lunge because my knees went out on me.

All at once I was so weak I couldn't stand up. I laid down and tried to catch my breath. Felt a little fuzzy in the head.

Pete was grinning, another indication that he didn't understand the seriousness of his situation. "Nice day for a walk, isn't it, Hankie?"

"Give me a minute to catch my breath and I'll show you how nice a day it is." Sure was feeling weak.

Pete yawned and stretched. "Tell me something, Hankie. With your eyes crossed, how will you find your way back home?"

"HUH?"

"I need to get back and finish your milk and eggs. You followed me out here but you won't be following me back. It might be hard to find the ranch."

Hadn't thought of it exactly in those terms. "Wait a minute, cat. *You* walked into *my* trap, so don't be trying to . . ."

"See you around, Hankie." He walked away, switching his tail and purring. He glanced back at me and winked. "If you need anything, just give me a call."

"Don't think you can bluff me, cat. Hey, come back here! Pete? Hey listen, I was only . . . let's talk this thing over . . . "

How the devil had I got myself in this mess?

As the afternoon wore on, I began to suspect that I was in a whole gob of trouble.

CHAPTER EIGHT

The Chopped Chicken Liver Mystery

~~~~~~

There's no pleasant way of describing my situation. I was in deep trouble, and with night coming on, it was getting deeper and deeper. Let's face it: the ranch was a dangerous place even in broad daylight, but at night, when the forces of darkness came out, it was no place for the faint-hearted.

When the sun slipped over the horizon, I felt the dampness rising from the ground and a shiver of dread passed through my battered carcass. Up the creek a ways, I heard the mournful hoot of an owl, and overhead the swish of a bull-bat's wings.

And little footsteps out there in the dark—mice, packrats, lizards, frogs, snakes, a guy didn't know what kind of creature might be creeping around out there, only I'll have to admit that snakes don't have feet so they don't take footsteps, but that's pretty creepy in itself, an animal that slithers and doesn't have the common decency to make a sound.

Me and snakes never did get along, just don't like 'em at all, the way they sneak and slither and slide and glide through the grass, and if I don't quit talking about snakes I'm going to get myself worked into a scare. No more about snakes.

There were no snakes out there slithering through the grass so that was one less thing I had to worry about, although I kept hearing this slithering sound out there in the grass. Sounded a lot like snakes, but I knew in my heart that it was big worms. I ain't scared of worms, even big ones.

I was feeling mighty small and helpless, curled up there in a ball with one ear perked up to monitor the sounds of the night, when all at once I heard a different kind of noise.

Heavy footsteps, the crackle of brush, the rumble of voices, and then . . . singing? Impossible. Nobody but a bunch of drunken coyotes would be singing at that hour of the night. I held my breath and listened.

> Me just a worthless coyote, me howling at
> the moon.
> Me like to sing and holler, me crazy as a
> loon.
> Me not want job or duties, no church or
> Sunday school,
> Me just a worthless coyote and me ain't
> nobody's fool.

Well, I certainly recognized that song, and I had a suspicion that I knew the guys who were singing it. Rip and Snort, the two coyote brothers.

I'd had some good times with those boys, back during my outlaw days, but I'd last seen them on the field of battle when I had single-handedly turned back an invasion of the entire coyote nation and saved the chickenhouse from a massacre.

I had some pretty fierce hand-to-hand combat with Rip and Snort, and I didn't figger they'd be real friendly if they caught me out there all by myself, half-blind and helpless.

I held my breath, hoping they would pass by. They came closer and closer. They were so busy singing and carrying on, I thought they'd miss me.

But all at once the singing stopped. Silence. I could hear my heart thumping. A twig snapped close by. I heard them whispering.

I turned my head around and looked into the sharp-nosed, yellow-eyed face of a coyote. "Well, if it isn't . . . I'll be derned . . . how in the world are you doing, Snort, by George it's great to see you boys again."

They stared at me.

"Been a long time, hasn't it?"

I could tell they were thinking.

"How's the family? How's old Scraunch getting along, just as ornery as ever, I bet."

They were still thinking. Rip and Snort were never what you'd call rapid thinkers.

"How come Hunk out here alone?"

"Alone? Well, that's . . . pretty obvious, isn't it? I mean . . . maybe it's not so obvious, huh?"

"Not so obvious."

I had a feeling that what I said here would be crucial to my survival. That's a lot of pressure, especially when you're in poor health.

"Well uh . . . fellers, I could tell you what I'm doing out here but you wouldn't believe it, I mean it's just the wildest craziest thing you ever heard in your life. You wouldn't believe it, would you?"

"Hear first, then decide."

"It'll take special powers of belief, and unless you guys think you can handle it, I'd rather not get into it."

They sat down. "Tell story," said Rip.

I glanced over both shoulders and lowered my voice. "Listen, I wouldn't be out here if this wasn't pretty derned special. I came alone because I didn't want anybody else to know about it. And if you should happen to pry this out of me, you've got to promise me three things."

They traded glances. "What promises?"

"First off, you've got to promise never to tell anyone about it. If news of this ever got out . . . well, it could be very serious. You promise never to tell?"

"We promise."

"All right, second thing is, you've got to follow the directions exactly and to the letter. One little mistake could cause a catastrophe."

Rip narrowed his eyes. "What means, catastrophe?"

"It means boom! Fire, explosion, black smoke in the sky, thunder and lightning, famine and drought, dead birds falling out of trees, the whole nine yards. You sure you want to know?"

They went into a huddle and talked it over. Then Snort said, "We take the chance."

"All right, now we're down to the last promise. You've got to promise to believe everything I tell you, no matter how crazy it sounds."

Snort shook his head. "Not work. Hear first, then decide. Snort not believe every crazy stuff that come along."

I was real sorry to hear that because the stuff I had in mind was pretty crazy. The brothers were getting restless. Snort got to his feet and stuck his sharp nose in my face.

"Better you tell or we have big fight, oh boy."

"All right, all right, relax. Look, Snort, you agreed to Promise Number Two, right? Promised to follow all the directions, right?"

"Right, that one okay."

"One of the directions is that you have to believe the story."

Snort and Rip looked at each other, and Snort said, "Uh."

"But I'll be reasonable about it. Since you've already agreed to believe the story, I'll drop the third promise. Would that make you feel better?"

Snort sat down and scratched his ear for a minute. "Very complicated, not quite understand."

"Yeah, but a promise is a promise. That's simple enough. What do you say, shall we scratch Number Three?"

Snort stared at me. "Scratch ear, got fleas."

"I mean, shall we drop Promise Number Three? That's the best I can do."

"We make talk." They went into a huddle and talked it over in whispers. Then Snort said, "Okay, we make deal. Drop Promise Three, keep One and Two."

"When it comes to driving a bargain, you guys are tough."

"We very tough, fighting a lot and singing coyote song."

"Well, are you ready for this?"

Their heads bobbed up and down. "We ready. "

"Then here goes. See that moon up there? Would you believe it's made of chopped chicken liver?" They shook their heads. "But you've already promised to believe it." They bobbed their heads up and down.

"Now, would you believe the moon can come down from the sky and land right here on the ground? And would you believe you can eat that chopped chicken liver until you bust?" They shook their heads. "But you already promised you'd believe it." They bobbed their heads up and down.

"And would you believe that if you two guys stuck your heads into opposite ends of a hollow log and counted to fifty thousand by ones, *it would make the moon come down?*"

Rip shook his head, but Snort raised his paw. "Ha! We already promise believe!" He looked at me and grinned. "Brother not catch on yet." And Rip nodded his head.

"Well, there you are, guys, now you know the whole story. But I hope you don't think I'm going to let you have the first shot at the chicken liver."

"Heh, Hunk not catch on either. Rip and Snort get whole moon, eat sick, throw up and eat some more, oh boy. Hunk good dog, sing pretty good, but not smart like coyote."

"Hey listen!" With great effort, I pushed myself up, and with very little effort, Snort pushed me back down.

"Stay here. Maybe we bring one liver. Now we find hollow log, count to many thousand. So long, Hunk."

"But what about . . . hey, wait . . ."

They plunged into the darkness, yipping and howling and laughing their heads off. I didn't waste a minute. I dragged myself down to the creek, slipped into a deep pool, and swam across to the other side.

I didn't want to be around come morning.

CHAPTER NINE

Invited for Breakfast

As you might have already figgered out by now, I went into the creek for two reasons: because it's easier to swim than to walk when you're stove up, and because you don't leave a scent in the water. I didn't want those two brothers following my scent.

I swam as far as I could, until the creek got too shallow, and then I climbed out and started walking. The swim must have done me some good because my aches and pains felt better when I got out. But I still had that Eye-Crosserosis problem, and I had no idea where I was going.

I walked until I came to a big cottonwood tree, and that's where I stopped for the night. Didn't sleep too soundly, kept having the same bad dream about getting whupped on my own ranch by a Doberman pinscher. Sounds familiar, don't it?

What woke me up was the sound of voices, two of them, and I knew that Rip and Snort had tracked me down and were fixing to stomp a mudhole in Hank the Cowdog. I just wasn't ready for that.

I opened my eyes and looked around. Couldn't see anyone, not even a blurred image of anyone. But then I heard the voices again, coming from the tree above me. I'd heard those voices before. They belonged to a couple of buzzards.

"Junior, you git outa that bed and go find us some breakfast!"

"But P-Pa . . ."

"It's shameful the way you mope around in the mornings. Why, when I was your age . . ."

"But P-Pa . . ."

". . . I was up every morning at daylight, yes I was, out looking for food. Do you want to know what your trouble is, son?"

"N-n-n-not really, not really."

"The trouble with you is you're lazy and shiftless, yes sir, and you seem to think our grub's gonna come walking up and park itself at the bottom of this tree. But life isn't that way, son, I've told you and I've told you."

"P-P-Pa?"

"What!"

"I th-think something w-w-walked up and p-p-p-p-parked itself at the bottom bottom bottom of this t-t-t-t-tree, tree, cause there's something dee-dee-duh-down there."

There was a long silence, then Wallace said, "And the other trouble with you, Junior, is that you have this smart-alecky streak. Nobody likes a smart aleck, son, what is that thang down there?"

"B-beats me, but it's g-g-got t-two tails and a ear."

"You mean two ears and a tail?"

"Th-that's what I su-su-su-said."

"You reckon it'll eat?"

"I bu-bet it will, 'cause I'm h-hungry."

"Follow me, son, and always remember that your elders get first dibs. I want a leg."

I glanced up and saw Wallace spread his wings and step off the branch. He flapped as hard as he could, but he must have miscalculated because he flew right into a tangle of grape-vines that were hanging on a big tree nearby. He squawked and flapped and tried to get out, but he got a leg caught and ended up hanging upside-down.

"Dang the luck! Now look what you've got me into!"

Junior stepped off the branch, flapped his wings, and crashed on the ground. The impact drove his beak into the dirt and he got up spitting.

"Junior! Get me down from here! Don't you dare take a bite, not one bite, until I get there."

Junior ignored him. He had a crazy grin on his face and came jumping toward me. I raised up and growled and showed him some fangs. He stopped in his tracks, and you should have seen that smile disappear. It just George melted.

"Oh d-d-darn!"

"Junior!" the old man yelled. "There's no call for cussin'. Now you just watch your language."

Junior turned and looked up at him. "Well, you c-c-cuss all the t-time."

"Son, there's a time for cussin' and a time for not cussin', and when you get old enough to know right from wrong, we'll let you try it, but there's no call for cussin' at this particular time, git me out of this tree!"

Junior glanced at me again. I gave him another growl and he edged a few steps away. "P-pa, it's hu-hu-hu-him again, him again, that same d-d-dog."

"What?"

"And he he he ain't du-dead again."

As I said, Wallace was hanging upside-down. He stared at me and I stared at him, and for good measure I gave 'em another growl.

"Well I'll be . . . of all the dad-danged, gosh-blamed, stinking, horrifying, son-of-a-gun pig-nosed lousy luck!"

"P-P-Pa? You're c-cussin'."

"You dang right I'm cussin'! When it's time to cuss, a guy needs to do it right, and furthermore, you git me out of this tree right now, you hear me, or I'll . . ."

"Y-you'll wha-wha-what, Pa?"

"I'll . . ." Just then his foot came loose and he crashed to the ground. ". . . be danged, like to of broke my neck, but you don't care, all you ever think about is yourself because the trouble with you, son, is that you've got no respect for age and wisdom, is what's wrong with you."

"I th-thought the tr-trouble with me was that . . ."

Wallace straightened his neck and came waddling over. "You got lots of troubles, is the trouble with you." He came over and glared down at me. "Shame on you!"

"Well, shame on you right back!"

That straightened him up. "Junior, did you

86

hear that? Are you gonna just stand there and take that off a dog?"

Junior peeked around the old man. "M-most likely I w-will, Pa, most l-likely, cause he m-m-might b-b-bite."

"Well, I never . . . when I was your age . . ." The old man rubbed his beak with the end of his wing and scowled. "Say there, neighbor, aren't you the same one who give us a chicken head one time?"

"Yep."

"I don't reckon you got another one."

"Nope."

"Didn't figger you did, sure could use one though."

Just then I had a brilliant idea. "Speaking of that chicken head, seems to me you boys promised to do me a favor some time."

The old man shook his head. "I don't recall that, sure don't."

"W-w-we did, Pa, w-we sure d-d-did."

Wallace snapped his head toward Junior. "And *you* can just *hush,* you don't have to tell everything you know!" Back to me. "Maybe we did, maybe we did."

"Well, I'm here to collect."

"Eh, what exactly did you have in mind, neighbor? We've had some bad luck lately and . . ."

I explained about the Eye-Crosserosis problem and how I was lost and couldn't find my way back to the ranch. All of a sudden Wallace seemed mighty interested.

"I see what you mean, yes. A guy could starve to death out here."

"I b-b-bet Madame M-Moonshine could f-f-f-fix his uh-uh-eyes, fix his eyes."

Me and the old man turned and stared at Junior, and I said, "Who's Madame Moonshine?"

"You hush your mouth, Junior, don't you . . ."

"She's a wu-wu-wu-witch and lives in a ca-ca-cave, in a cave."

"She's a witch? And lives in a cave?"

"No, she's no such thing," Wallace butted in, "and she don't live in no cave, and Junior you leave the talking to me, and as for you," he looked at me, "we can't help you."

I got to my feet and went nose-to-nose with the old man. "Listen, you old bucket of guts, I gave you a chicken head and I'm fixing to collect a *buzzard's* head unless you take me to Madame Moonshine. Pronto."

"Well, you don't have to be so tacky about it. I just thought, see what you done, Junior?"

"I d-done right, P-Pa, cause he's our f-friend."

"Friend," Wallace muttered. "The only friend

a buzzard's got is his next meal. Wouldn't hurt you to remember that."

Wallace went waddling through the willows, still grumbling to himself, and me and Junior fell in behind him.

Up ahead, I could hear Wallace carrying on: ". . . danged kids . . . tried to tell the boy . . . stubborn, mule-headed . . . never amount to bird hockey . . ."

It was quite a procession, two waddling buzzards and one jake-legged dog. As we walked along, Junior told me about Madame Moonshine. Said she was a burrowing owl, used to live in a prairie dog town (which is where you find most burrowing owls, don't you see), only the prairie dogs ran her out of town because she had a witchy kind of power.

Sounded pretty strange to me.

We picked our way through the willows, until at last we came to a rocky ledge on the south bank of the creek. Wallace stopped and pointed to a cave.

"There it is. This is as far as we go. She's in there somewhere."

I turned to Junior. "You sure this is the right thing to do?"

"I b-b-bet she can f-fix you."

"Well, thanks again." I started up the ledge. When I went past the old man, he curled his lip at me.*

"G-G-Good luck," Junior called. "And w-wwatch out for the s-s-s-snakes!"

"HUH?"

"Rattlesnakes," said Wallace, "dozens of 'em, place is crawling with 'em. And say, if you get bit, try to make it outside the cave before you die, would you? I'd like for something to come of this friendship."

I tried to think of a brilliant reply, something slashing and witty that would really put the old bird in his place. Sometimes I can come up with brilliant replies and sometimes I can't. This time I couldn't.

I headed for the cave, feeling just a little shaky about them snakes, not to mention the witch. I'd never met a witch before.

---

* Some bird experts would probably point out here that buzzards don't have lips, so Wallace couldn't have curled his lip at me. Okay, maybe he didn't, but he did something with his beak that certainly gave that impression.

H.C.D.

CHAPTER TEN

Madame Moonshine

I climbed the ledge and stuck my head into the cave, sniffed, checked things out. It looked suspicious to me.

I'm not the kind of dog who enjoys holes. Some do, I guess, but not me. I got locked into a big wooden tack box when I was a kid, and since then I've tried to avoid places that are dark and closed in.

I started inside the cave, got a creepy feeling, and backed out. Figgered I'd better study on it a little more before I did anything drastic. I mean, Junior had said something about snakes, and you know where I stand on the snake issue.

How did I know that Madame Moonshine could cure Eye-Crosserosis? In fact, how did I know that Madame Moonshine even existed? All I had to go on was the word of a couple of buzzards, and in the security business we tend to give low priority to the testimony of buzzards.

I'd just about talked myself out of going in there when I realized I had some company. I was peering inside the cave, see, and happened to glance to my left and saw a little owl—a burrowing owl, in fact, which I thought was an interesting coincidence. She was peering into the cave too.

"What's in there?" she whispered. She had big yellow eyes, and I noticed she had a way of rolling her head around without moving her body.

"I don't know, ma'am. I've been told that someone called Madame Moonshine hangs out here. I don't suppose you know anything about her, do you? They say she's a witch or something."

The lady's head twisted around and she stared at me with them big eyes. "You believe in witches?"

"Well, I don't know for sure. Never met one."

"I don't believe in them, and I've met several. But I don't believe in dogs either, so there you are."

"How come you don't believe in dogs? I mean, I'm a dog myself."

"Well, that's only your opinion. Everyone has an opinion."

I couldn't help chuckling at that. "Yeah, but I'm Head of Ranch Security, see. Maybe you didn't realize that. You might say that I run this ranch, so my opinion carries a little weight."

"Ah! So *you* run this ranch?"

"Yes ma'am, and have for several years. There's very little that goes on around here without my say-so."

"I see. Do you make the sun rise?"

"Uh . . . not exactly. "

"Do you tell the trees when to shed their leaves?"

"Well . . . no.

"Did you teach the fish to swim?"

"No ma'am."

She bent down and looked at the ground. "There's an ant. Would you mind telling him to go somewhere else?"

I was feeling a little uncomfortable about this. "I guess I could try. Ant, scram, go on, get out of here!" It didn't work.

The lady gave me a puzzled look. "Now tell me again: what is it that you do?"

"I'm Head of . . . look, ants don't listen to anybody, they just ain't smart enough."

Now get this. She spread out her wings and brought them together in front, so they pointed toward the ant, and she made a kind of whistling sound. The derned fool ant stopped in his tracks, turned around, and ran away.

The lady looked at me and grinned and blinked her eyes. "I'm sorry, what were you saying?"

"Nuthin'." Then all at once it struck me. All the clues came together. I had figgered it out. "Wait a minute! I bet you're Madame Moonshine."

"Oh yes I am! And you're Hank the Rabbit."

"Huh? No, I'm Hank the Cowdog."

"Of course! Yes, I see now. Won't you come in?"

I squinted into that dark hole and gave it another sniffing. "You got any snakes in there?"

"How many did you want?"

"I don't want any, I'm scared of 'em."

"Oh rubbish, just tell them who you are. Come, follow me."

She hopped into the hole. I swallered real hard and went in behind her. It was pretty narrow and it got dark all of a sudden. I'd gone five or six feet when I started hearing a bunch of hissing and rattling and felt cold things crawling around.

It was them dadgum snakes. I couldn't turn around, I couldn't back out, so I crawled forward just as fast as I could. For a while I could hear Madame Moonshine hopping in front of me, but then all I could hear was hissing and rattling.

"Ma'am?" No answer. I began to suspect that I'd made an error in judgment. I mean, Eye-Crosserosis is pretty bad stuff, but it beats the heck out of Dead-Doggerosis.

The cave turned to the left, and up ahead I could see a big chamber with a shaft of sunlight coming down. I crawled toward it as fast as I could.

I was out of breath when I got there, and when I looked around there was no sign of Madame Moonshine. I sat down and waited. Heard a sound off to my left, turned, and saw a huge, enormous diamondback rattlesnake slipping toward me. He was flicking his tongue out and he had a wicked look in his eyes.

My first instinct was to build a new door in the roof, but then I remembered what Madame Moonshine had said. I held my ground and tried to get control of the shakes.

"I'm Hank the Cowdog," I said in my gruffest voice, "Head of Ranch Security." He kept coming. "Maybe you didn't hear me. I said I'm Hank the Cowdog, Head of Ranch Security."

That was supposed to do the trick, but it didn't. The snake built a coil at my feet and started buzzing.

I thought I was finished, fellers, but just then

Madame Moonshine's head popped out of a hole in the cave wall. "Back again! Oh, you've met Timothy, and my goodness, I think he's going to bite you. Didn't you tell him who you are? Timothy, shame on you! Go away, shoo! This is the *Head of Ranch Security.*"

The snake slipped away into the gloom. She came out of the hole in the wall and hopped over to the place where the sunlight hit the floor. "Now, tell me why you're here."

I told her the whole story, about how my eyes had crossed and how Rufus had whupped up on me, how Pete had suckered me out into the wilderness, the buzzards, everything.

While I told the story, she picked up a lizard bone in her claws and chewed on it, and every now and then she would give her head a nod.

"You think you can help me, Madame?"

She pitched the bone aside and wiped her mouth on her wing. "Maybe and maybe not. We'll have to test you. How many fingers am I holding up?"

I squinted at her. "Uh . . . three?"

"No! I'm holding NO fingers up. Owls HAVE no fingers. Can you read the letters on this chart?"

I squinted again. "Ma'am, I can't even see the derned chart."

"Good! Excellent! There isn't one. Now, can you tell me the color of this tree?"

You can fool Hank the Cowdog once in a row or maybe twice in a row but not three times. "There's no tree, ma'am."

"There certainly IS a tree! This is the bottom part, called a root. It's brown. Yes, you have a problem, but I just happen to have a cure."

"You do?"

"I certainly do! Come over here, lie down, and hold still."

I did as she said. She closed her eyes and took

the end of my nose in her claws. I watched her very carefully and memorized every step, and what you're about to hear is the secret combination that will cure Eye-Crosserosis. Here's what she said, word for word:

"Left, two." She twisted my nose twice to the left. "Right, three." She twisted it right three times. "Left, one . . . and push!"

I don't expect anyone to believe this, but it's the by-George truth. When she pushed my nose, my tail shot up, my mouth fell open, and my eyes came uncrossed.

I told you you wouldn't believe it.

I could see again! Everything was clear! Madame Moonshine stepped back and smiled. "Oh, it worked! How nice! But to be sure, let's test it. How many legs do I have?"

"Two."

"Excellent! How many wings?"

"Uh . . . two?"

"Ver-ry good! Now just one last question. How do you expect to get out of here?"

"HUH? Well uh . . . I sort of thought you might lead me out and keep the snakes down, is sort of what I thought."

She shook her head. "Oh dear. You missed that one."

I glanced around and saw big Timothy coiled in the middle of my escape route. "What's the correct answer?"

She clapped her wings together. "The correct answer is that you'll stay and we'll play riddles—for days and days and weeks and weeks and years and years and ever and ever, until you solve one, and then," she shrugged, "I shall have to let you go."

"Now hold on. I've got a job."

"Rubbish."

"I've got responsibilities."

"Rubbish."

"I need to get back."

"Rubbish."

"And I'm gonna leave one way or . . ."

"Timothy?"

Big Tim started buzzing.

"On second thought, let's play riddles."

"Oh good! Here's one: if wishes were horses, beggars would be . . . what?"

"Uh . . . cowboys?"

"No."

"Saddles?"

"No."

"I really do need to get back, Madame Moon-shine."

She laid down and propped her head up on her

wing. "But you can't, Hank. I'm a witch and I can't stand for things to be simple. There must be a non-reason for everything. I can't just let you leave without a non-reason. No, you'll have to answer a riddle before I can let you go."

I studied Big Tim again. He flicked out his tongue. "Okay, let's hit the riddles."

"Here's a good one: How much wood could a woodpecker chuck if a peckerwood's a checkerboard square?" I asked her to repeat it. "How much wood could a woodpecker chuck if a peckerwood's a checkerboard square?"

I said it over. "Can you give me a hint?"

"Just one hint. The answer's not what you think it is."

"That's a big help. Well, give me a minute. I'll have to do some figgering."

I had to use some algebra on this one. I mean, when you go to multiplying woodpeckers times peckerwoods and adding in all the chucks and chips and checkerboards, you've got to have some pretty stout mathematics. Plain old numbers won't work.

I figgered and I figgered. I wrote all my formulas in the dust, scratched out one or two, added a number here and a formula there, and finally came up with the answer.

Madame Moonshine was wearing a peculiar smile.

"Okay, here we are. The answer I get is 5.03."

The bottom fell out of her smile. "I don't believe it!" She sat up and stared at me. "No one has ever solved that riddle before! How did you do it?"

"Well, ma'am, all I can say is that they didn't make me Head of Ranch Security for nothing. I have certain talents, I guess."

"That," she said in a low voice, "is a monstrous understatement. You could very well be a genius!"

"You're not the first one that's said that, ma'am."

"I can imagine not!" She closed her eyes and clasped her wings together. "Oh dear, I shall have to let you go. Timothy? Open!"

The snake crawled over into a corner. Madame Moonshine sighed and led the way. On the way out, I could hear them snakes crawling around, and I was mighty glad Madame was leading the way.

When we reached the opening, I stepped outside. I looked around and I could see again!

"Well, ma'am, I want to thank you for everything. You've done this ranch a tremendous favor, and we'll never forget it. Bye now."

I trotted down the hill. " Oh Hank?" she called.

I stopped and turned back to her. "Do you believe in witches now?"

I had to chuckle at that. "Yes ma'am, I reckon I do. And do you believe in dogs now?"

She thought about that for a second. "No." And with that, she was gone.

Instead of going back to the ranch, I headed down the creek. I had a little errand to take care of on the next ranch.

CHAPTER ELEVEN

War!

It was three miles to the ranch where Plato and Beulah and Rufus stayed. I kept to the creek for a mile or so and then got up on the county road when the creek made its big horseshoe bend to the north.

Boy, I felt good! The air was sweet with wild-flowers and the sunshine warmed my back. My eyes worked, my aches and pains had gone away, and I could feel the muscles inside my skin, straining to get out and do handsprings.

I made a mental note to myself: "Next time you get to feeling poorly, go see Madame Moonshine because she can cure more ills than Black Draught."

(I knew about Black Draught because Loper

once used it to cure me of a case of worms. Don't try it unless everything else has failed and it's come down to a choice between Black Draught and certain death.)

It was late afternoon when I reached the outbuildings of the ranch and by that time I had worked out my strategy. Instead of busting in and having a showdown right away, I would lurk around and check things out. Also give my highly conditioned body a chance to recharge.

I didn't want to underestimate the magnitude of the task before me. Taking on Rufus would be a handful, even on a good day.

I went creeping through some tall grass on the west edge of the place. I could see Billy down at the corrals, working with a young horse. Didn't see any signs of Beulah or Rufus.

I spotted a pile of old cedar posts and headed for it. I would set up a scout position there and just, you know, let the pot bubble for a while.

I reached the post pile and was peering around a corner when I heard a noise. Sounded like . . . it was kind of hard to describe, but it sounded a whole lot like teeth chattering. And it was coming from inside the pile. I cocked my head and listened.

"Who's in there?"

"Nobody," said a squeaky voice.

"Huh, you expect me to believe that? You ain't dealing with just any old slouch. You'd best come out before I get riled."

"Who are you?"

"Who I am is irrelevant. The order is for you to come out before I have to make kindling out of this post pile."

"Okay, I'm coming, but don't bite for Pete's sake, my skin tears very easily!"

Out came a spotted bird dog with rings around his eyes that made it appear that he was wearing glasses. He was trembling all over. You guessed it: Plato, my old rival in the love-of-Beulah department. We'd met once or twice before, but we weren't what you'd call bosom friends.

"Hank? Oh thank heaven it's you!"

"It may be too soon to thank heaven, Plato."

He slapped his paw against his cheek. "At first I thought you were that Doberman. This has been an incredible experience. Would you believe five days in the post pile, I mean actually in fear of my *life*! I'm telling you, man, it's been . . ."

"Where's Rufus?"

Plato's eyes widened. "I don't know where Rufus is, and that's okay. I've got nothing at all against the dog. I'm perfectly willing to relate to him . . . why do you ask?"

"I'm looking for him."

"Good heavens! Why?"

"Grudge."

"Grudge? Okay." He started backing toward the post pile. "Well, my position is very simple, Hank."

"Your position better stay out of the post pile."

"Sure, okay, but what I'm saying is that I don't really approve of grudges, the idea, I mean."

"This ain't an idea."

He nodded. "Okay."

I peered around the edge of the post pile and studied the lay of the land. Then I caught sight of the enemy. He was down in the back yard, chewing on a big steak bone. Beulah sat a few feet away, watching him tear at the bone.

"Come here, Plato, and take a look."

He crept over and peeked around the corner. "Good heavens! Just look at him!"

"Here's the way I figger it. You'll go down first and get his attention . . ."

"What!"

". . . and I'll move out and keep under cover. While he's busy with you, I'll attack and hit him on the blind side."

"Wait a minute, Hank."

"I hate to take a cheap shot, but I got a feeling

we're gonna need the element of surprise."

"Hey listen, Hank, I think we've got a basic misunderstanding here. What I have in mind is more of an advisory role, you see the distinction? I mean, I think my talents . . . listen, man, that dog is *terrible*! Do you have any idea what he can do with those teeth?"

"Got a real good idea, Plato. That's why I need a decoy."

"Decoy, is it? You mean a sitting duck. No way am I going down there to . . ." I turned on my slow rumble of a growl. Plato swallowed and blinked his eyes. "You're giving me no choice, is that it?"

"Yep."

"Suicide, that's what you're asking. Ho, what madness!" He began marching up and down in front of me. "You've spent years cultivating your mind, Plato, training yourself to hunt birds. Now all we ask is that you offer yourself to the dragon, to be torn into ribbons of quivering, bleeding flesh!"

"You finished?"

He stopped. "Yes, I am finished, in every sense of the word. However, if I might offer one small suggestion, suppose we held me in reserve . . ."

"Get going."

"Very well, all right, fine. But I must warn

you: if I am maimed or disfigured, I shall hold you personally responsible."

"Hit the road."

"History will be your judge, Hank. Unborn generations of bird dogs will . . ."

I gave him a shove and got him out of there. I mean, he could have gone on yapping for the rest of the afternoon. I still had some work to do.

Rufus heard the commotion and looked up from his bone. He watched Plato walk down the hill, and a grin spread across his face. Beulah saw him too, and her mouth dropped open.

Rufus pushed himself up. "Ha ha! Fresh meat!"

"Listen, Rufus," yelled Plato, "I can explain everything. Try to control yourself for just a minute and hear me out. We've had a little misunderstanding here but I'm convinced that we can talk it over . . ."

"Watch my bone, honey." Rufus started dragging his paws across the ground.

"Leave him alone, Rufus, he hasn't done anything!"

"He's alive, and I take that as a personal insult." He rolled his muscular shoulders and stepped out toward Plato.

The trap was set. I slipped away from the post

pile and started creeping down the hill, taking cover behind shrubs and trash cans.

Plato started edging back toward the post pile. "We're in basic agreement on most issues, Rufus, except that . . ."

"I can't stand your face." Rufus was stalking him now, coming closer to the spot where I was waiting.

"Right, exactly, which is basically a superficial . . ."

All at once Rufus sprang into a lope. The muscles in his shoulders and thighs rippled. His teeth were bared and his little eyes glistened. All the world had narrowed down to Plato and that's all he could see.

I shot one last glance at Beulah, coiled my legs under me, and exploded out of the shrubs.

Plato stood on rubber legs and started babbling. ". . . can talk this thing out, Rufus, don't look at me that way, I can explain, don't tear my skin!"

There's a kind of evil beauty about a Doberman pinscher who's moving in for the kill, a kind of gracefulness that sparkles when he's got murder on his mind. I caught a little glimpse of that, and then I hit him.

Old Rufus never saw me coming, never had

the slightest notion that he'd wandered into my trap. I hit him with a full head of steam, which was important because I knew I'd have to stun him with a good lick or he'd come back and we don't need to go into that.

I put a real stunner on him, got a clamp on his neck and rode him to the ground. We rolled and kicked and snarled and ripped, sent up a big cloud of dust, tore up grass and weeds, and if I'm not mistaken, I think we even broke off a huge tree.

That gives you some idea of just how terrible a battle it was: I mean, things were flying through the air, the dust got so thick I could hardly breathe, tree limbs were falling to the ground.

Well, I gnawed on one of Rufus's ears and had things pretty muchly under control when, dern the luck, he put that same judo move on me, I should have been watching for it, got too preoccupied with the ear, and all at once he had me flat on the ground.

Then he hit right in the middle of me, kind of knocked the breath out of me.

I could hear Plato. "Sock him, Hank, knock his eye out! Give him one for me! Watch out, no, no, no, for Pete's sake, don't let him throw you, bad move, Hank, real poor move, you've got to keep the upper hand, use your teeth, man!"

"Get in here, you idiot, before he kills us all!" I managed to holler.

Just then Beulah got there. Never thought I'd need the help of a damsel in distress; did though. She jumped astraddle his back and although she wasn't real big, she started reading him the riot act.

And then, to the surprise of heaven and earth and all God's wonderful creation, Plato hopped in. On a good day, he might be mean enough to chew up a wet Kleenex—maybe—but at least he was there and added a little weight to the pile. I was able to get one paw free and delivered a good stroke to Rufus's nose.

We got him on the ground and then playtime started. I was in the process of whupping the ever-living tar out of Roof-Roof when Billy came running down from the corral, yelling and waving his arms. His face was deep red.

"Hyah, get outa here! Hank, you sorry devil, go home!"

The rocks started flying. Plato and Beulah scattered for the post pile. I figgered I'd hang around for one more lick when I caught a stone in the upper back, hurt like the very dickens, and decided to evacuate.

I stepped off. "See you around, Roofie."

Billy chunked another rock that zinged past my ear, so I loped up to the post pile.

"Don't you ever come back here!" Billy yelled. "Just let me get my gun . . ."

I ducked behind the posts. Beulah and Plato were there. She came up to me and nuzzled my chin. "You were just great, Hank!"

"Incredible, Hank, terrific job!"

They were right, of course, but you can't come

out and say that. "Y'all didn't do so bad your-selves."

Beulah peeked around the corner and motioned for us to take a look. Billy was standing over his famous fighting dog and preaching him some hot gospel.

". . . two hundred bucks and then you get yourself whipped by a ten-ninety-five, flea-bitten, sewer-dipping cowdog!" (He was referring to me, by the way.) "I oughta just take you to town and find some other sucker . . ."

Never saw old Roof look so humble. Even them high-toned ears seemed a trifle wilted.

We held a little celebration there behind the post pile, then Beulah said, "You'd better go, Hank. Billy's mad enough to shoot you."

"When you're made of steel, you don't worry about lead."

Plato nodded. "Well put, Hank, very well put."

Beulah only smiled—that wonderful smile of hers that said, "You're probably one of the greatest dogs in the world and I'm about to fall helplessly in love with you but you'd better go," or something to that effect.

Anyway, she leaned up and kissed me on the cheek, which sent ripples of joy clean out to the end of my tail. "Good-bye, Hank."

So I loped off toward the creek and into the sunset. Just before I disappeared from sight, I stopped and gave 'em one last wave.

They waved back, which was fine and dandy, but when Plato lowered his paw, it came to rest on Beulah's shoulder. And instead of slugging him in the teeth, as she should have done, she let it stay there.

Moral #1: Time heals some wounds but makes others worse.

Moral #2: Women are hard to figger out.

Moral #3: Women are impossible to figger out.

Moral #4: Might as well give up trying.

Home Again

It was dark by the time I got into familiar country again. Off to the north I could see the caprock brooding in the moonlight, and off to the south I could hear the bullfrogs croaking along the creek. Up ahead, I could see the dark outline of the machine shed.

I'd been gone for days and I had notched up some pretty exciting adventures, but it would be good to be back home again.

I wondered how tight the security had been in my absence. I had a pretty good idea, but I decided to give it a little test. Instead of coming into headquarters the back way, I marched right past the house and the machine shed, the vital center of the ranch operation.

No challenge, no warning, no order to halt, no barking, no nuthin'. I mean, the whole place was exposed like an open wound. Any scoundrel could have walked in there and had himself a picnic.

I went on down to the gas tanks to see if Drover, my assistant head of non-security, was pushing up Z's on his gunnysack. He wasn't there, so I moved on down to the corral. As I approached the saddle shed, I heard voices and slowed to a stealthy walk. I kept close to the fence and crept up to where I could see and hear.

"I'm tired of playing tag," said Pete.

"And I'm tired of chasing crickets. I kind of miss old Hank, don't you?"

Pete's head came up. "Hank. Now there's an idea."

Drover looked around. "Where?"

"Why don't we put on a play?"

"A play? What do you mean?"

"I'll be Hank and you be Rufus. We'll make it a comedy on Hankie."

"A comedy? You mean . . . we'll make fun of him?"

"Something like that." Pete flicked the end of his tail back and forth and rubbed against the post. "Now, wouldn't that be fun?"

"Well . . . it might be. But I bet Hank wouldn't appreciate it."

"Of course he would. You know what a wonderful sense of humor he has."

"I do?"

"Certainly! If he has a single fault, it's that he's always making jokes at his own expense."

"Hank does that?"

Pete went over and started waving his tail in front of Drover's eyes. The little mutt's head went back and forth in time with it. "And besides, Hankie's not around, remember? We can do *anything* we want, and what he doesn't know won't hurt him."

Drover glanced over his shoulder. "I don't know about that."

"Just watch the tail, Drover. Keep your eyes on the tip. That's better. Think of how much fun it would be." Pete was purring now. He brought the tip of his tail under Drover's chin and wound it around his nose.

"Maybe so. You don't think it would be . . . disrespectful, do you?"

"My heavens no! All you have to do is play Rufus. I'll do Hankie's lines. Just try to imagine that you're a Doberman pinscher."

"Well, all right . . . if you're sure . . . I just hope Hank doesn't catch us."

Pete rubbed on Drover's leg. "No one will be

any the wiser. Now, make up your lines in verse and get into character. Here, watch me. I'll do the Hank-walk."

He puffed himself up and started swaggering around. Struck me as a real poor acting job. I mean, it was perfectly obvious that he wasn't imitating ME. What we had there was a classic example of how a dumb cat can play a dumb part and still come out looking dumb.

"And you see," said Pete, "I've got my eyes crossed and I'll start running into things."

Drover tried not to laugh. "That's not very nice . . . but it is kind of funny."

Pete ran into a post, grabbed his nose, yowled, and rolled over on his back. "You're on, Rufus, say your lines."

Drover walked over to him, kind of stiff-legged, and here are the immortal words that came out of his mouth:

My name is Roof and I've come with proof
That cowdogs are a silly invention.
Now get off the ground, let's go round and
    round
And chew on my bone of contention.

Pete grinned and nodded. "Ver-ry good, ver-ry good! You're a blooming poet, Drover. Do some more, only this time make it a little . . ." He studied his claws. *"Nastier."*

"Well, I don't know . . . I guess I could try . . . let's see here:

I'm a Doberman pinscher and I don't wear
    dentures,
I'm big and I'm mean and I'm rude.
You think you're hot stuff, so get off your duff.
Hot stuff is my favorite food.

"EX-cellent, excellent!" Pete tapped his paws together. "You're getting the hang of it now."

Drover gave a silly grin and wagged his stub tail. "You don't think it was too nasty, do you, Pete?"

"It's only a play. It's not real."

"I guess you're right but . . ."

"Now it's time for my part. Enter Hankie." Pete did his blind stagger routine again, puffed himself up and bounced off a couple of fenceposts:

Sir Hankie's my name and protection's my
     game,
I usually stay angry and wroth.
I bet halitosis would beat crosserosis,
But dang it, I think I've got both!

Drover covered his mouth with a paw but couldn't keep from laughing. "Oh, that's terrible, that's just . . . can you do some more?"

"You like that, hmmm? Give me a minute to think."

While he was thinking I figgered it might be a good time for me to say MY part. I had an idea it would bring down the house:

My name is Drover, your little play's over,
Beware all you cats and dumb mutts.

You've had your good fun and now you'd best
run
'Cause I'm fixing to start kicking butts!

I stood up. All eyes were on me. Pete quit flicking his tail. "Hmmm. The cops are here."

Drover gasped and squeaked. "Oh my gosh I knew we shouldn't . . . hi Hank . . . Pete made me . . . I told him . . ."

Pete started edging down the fence toward the feed barn. "Well, I think I'll do a little mouse patrol."

I turned on my incredible speed and in three jumps I had him rolled up into a hissing, spitting ball of fur. Drover started jumping up and down. "Git 'im, Hankie, git 'im!"

I gave the cat a pretty sound thrashing before he slipped out of my grip and made a dash for the feed barn. There's a hole at the bottom of the door, just big enough for a cat to slither through and not quite big enough for a dog.

Pete made a run for it, one step ahead of my jaws. He made it through the hole and I figgered, what the heck, I might as well tear the door down, so I lowered my head and rammed it into the hole.

Turned out the door was a little stouter than I'd thought, cricked up my neck pretty severely, and boy was I surprised when I couldn't get my head out of the hole. Had to throw everything into reverse and plow with all four paws before she popped free.

Drover was still hopping up and down. "Atta way, Hankie, nice work, boy we taught that cat!" I straightened my neck up and marched over to him. He quit hopping around and studied me. "Hank?" I kept marching, didn't say a word, and in a flash little Drover was highballing it up the hill to the machine shed.

I took out after him, figgered I'd catch him about halfway up the hill, only little Drover is faster than you might suppose when he knows his life's in danger. Never did catch the runt. He disappeared inside the machine shed.

"You might as well come out, Drover," I said, peering into the darkness and trying to decide which stack of junk he was hiding behind: the paint cans, the windmill parts, the old tires, the electric fence batteries, the spare parts for the stock trailer, High Loper's canoe, Sally May's wedding presents—you could have lost three elephants in that place. "Come on, Drover, and face the music. I see you."

"We was only funnin', Hank, it wasn't real. Pete said so."

"You coming out or do I have to tear this place apart?"

"I'm scared, Hank."

"Okay, you asked for it."

I waded in. When something got in my way, I just by George leveled it, knocked it aside, left it in rubble. You should have heard them paint cans clatter! I mean, when Hank the Cowdog gets on a case, nothing's safe, especially a villain. It's only a matter of time until I track him down and then you can imagine the terrible scene.

Drover was in real peril.

I tore the place apart, turned it upside-down, just about wore me out. "Drover, tell you what I'm gonna do. If you'll turn yourself in, we'll forget the death penalty. I'll let you off with a good thrashing."

"I'm still scared, Hank. I'm too scared to walk."

"All right, a minor thrashing."

"I'm just petrified, Hank, I can't move."

I thought for a long time. Justice has to be flexible. "Okay, here's my last offer. If you'll stand with your nose in the corner for fifteen minutes, we'll let it slide this time."

He came out. He'd been under the canoe. Sure thought he was behind the paint cans. "Now you march down to the gas tanks and put your nose in the corner."

"Okay, Hank, but that's a terrible punishment."

"You bet it is, and let this be a lesson to you."

We picked our way through the junk, across the cement floor to the door. When we got into the moonlight, Drover stopped. "Oh my gosh, Hank, look at you feet! You're bleeding!"

I glanced down. Sure 'nuff, my feet were covered with blood. Must have cut them on something sharp and terrible. I started getting faint from loss of blood. My legs got wobbly. "Rush me to the sewer, Drover, this is serious."

Drover sniffed the air. "Wait a minute. What's that I smell?"

Just before I lost consciousness, I sniffed the air. "Wait a minute. What's that I smell? It's paint, Drover, red paint. You saw something red and wet and jumped to conclusions. A lot of times you can study the clues, son, and figger these things out. Now march."

I marched him down to the gas tanks and stuck his nose in the corner. It was a terrible punishment, all right, but he had it coming.

Well, it was great to be home again. I mean, in just a few days' time, I'd managed to get all the loose ends tied together. I had my ranch back in order and things were running smoothly again.

Just to give you an idea of how well things worked out, around seven o'clock in the morning I looked up in the sky and saw the silver monster bird again, but he wasn't flying low this time, no siree, he was way the heck up there. I mean, you scare them birds bad enough and they'll stay off your ranch. They know the meaning of danger.

I was watching the monster bird pass over when I heard High Loper and Slim coming down the hill. I looked around and was shocked to see a smile on Loper's face. And unless I was badly mistaken, he was even laughing to himself.

"Hank, by golly, I just heard the good news. Billy called, and boy, was he steamed up! Said you gave his Doberman a licking. Heck of a deal, heck of a deal!" He whopped me on the side a couple of times, made me cough in fact, but that was okay. "This calls for a celebration. Double dog food, Hankie, come on boy, let's go up to the machine shed."

Off we went: a loyal, courageous dog and his master. It was just by George a pretty touching moment in ranch history.

But as you might expect, Drover tried to butt in—you know, as if he had done something to deserve special commendation, when in fact he was still on probation.

"You stay here, son, and think about doing right for a change."

Loper chuckled all the way up the hill. "Just went over there and whipped that old Doberman, on his own ranch! I like that, Hank, shows spunk and spirit and vinegar and . . ."

We had walked into the machine shed. Loper stopped. His smile began to droop, then it fell flat. He walked to the center of the room. Slim and I waited at the doorway. The place was . . . well, a little messy, shall we say.

His eyes went to the paint cans and the big

puddle of red on the floor. He looked at the red tracks on the cement. He looked at my red paws. I glanced around to cast an accusing eye at Drover, but naturally the little dunce wasn't paying me any mind.

I began to wag my tail.

I can't see that it would serve any purpose to go into details here. It should be clear by now that the machine shed was damaged in the line of duty. It should be clear that misunderstanding is just one of the prices of greatness.

Those of us who live on the heights must live with the judgments of small minds. We can only hope that in the next life justice will reign.

It reigns here, but it also hails.

Have you read all of Hank's adventures?

Join Hank the Cowdog's Security Force

Are you a big Hank the Cowdog fan? Then you'll want to join Hank's Security Force. Here is some of the neat stuff you will receive:

Welcome Package
- A Hank paperback embossed with Hank's top secret seal
- Free Hank bookmarks

Eight issues of *The Hank Times* with
- Stories about Hank and his friends
- Lots of great games and puzzles
- Special previews of future books
- Fun contests

More Security Force Benefits
- Special discounts on Hank books and audiotapes
- An original Hank poster (19" x 25") absolutely free

Total value of the Welcome Package and *The Hank Times* is $23.95. However, your two-year membership is **only $8.95** plus $3.00 for shipping and handling.

☐ Yes I want to join Hank's Security Force. Enclosed is $11.95 ($8.95 + $3.00 for shipping and handling) for my **two-year membership**. [Make check payable to Maverick Books.]

Which book would you like to receive in your Welcome Package? Choose from books 1–30.

(#   )   (#   )

FIRST CHOICE   SECOND CHOICE

BOY or GIRL

YOUR NAME   (CIRCLE ONE)

MAILING ADDRESS

CITY   STATE   ZIP

TELEPHONE   BIRTH DATE

E-MAIL

Are you a ☐ Teacher or ☐ Librarian?

Send check or money order for $11.95 to:

Hank's Security Force
Maverick Books
PO Box 549
Perryton, Texas 79070

DO NOT SEND CASH. NO CREDIT CARDS ACCEPTED.
Allow 4–6 weeks for delivery.

The Hank the Cowdog Security Force, the Welcome Package, and The Hank Times *are the sole responsibility of Maverick Books. They are not organized, sponsored, or endorsed by Penguin Putnam Inc., Puffin Books, Viking Children's Books, or their subsidiaries or affiliates.*